Have you read the other books in the series?

Olivia's First Term
Olivia Flies High
Olivia's Enchanted Summer
Olivia's Winter Wonderland
Olivia and the Great Escape
Olivia's Curtain Call

"Hugely enjoyable"
The Stage

"Gripping"

Olivia
and the
Movie Stars

Olivia looked at the text message. She really wanted to believe that Katie had changed, but she'd been fooled by her before. She *was* curious, though. What information could Katie have that would be of interest to her? She hesitated for a second, then pressed the delete button.

Olivia

and the
Movie Stars

LYN GARDNER

nosy
crow

First published in the UK in 2012 by Nosy Crow Ltd
The Crow's Nest, 10a Lant Street
London, SE1 1QR, UK

Nosy Crow and associated logos are trademarks and/or registered
trademarks of Nosy Crow Ltd

A CIP catalogue record for this book will be available from the
British Library.

Printed and bound in the UK by Clays Ltd, St. Ives Plc
Typeset by Tiger Media Ltd, Bishops Stortford, Hertfordshire

Papers used by Nosy Crow are made from wood grown in
sustainable forests.

ISBN: 978 0 85763 026 1

www.nosycrow.com

Chapter One

"How very odd," said Georgia, leaning out of the dance studio window on the second floor of The Swan Academy of Theatre and Dance. "There are three people with cameras hiding in the bushes down by the front steps. Do you think we should tell Miss Swan?"

"Let me see," said Tom, jumping off the high-wire. He brushed back his red hair and ran over to the window. He gave a little whistle. "Georgia's right. And there's another one sitting in that blue BMW across the street. The Swan's being staked out by the paparazzi!" he said excitedly. "Someone famous must be coming to visit."

The children were used to celebrities visiting the Swan. Often they were ex-pupils.

Hot magazine had recently done a photo-feature about the princess of pop, Amber Lavelle, returning to her former school, and at the end of last term Theo Deacon – whose performance at the National Theatre was dubbed by the critics as "a Hamlet to die for" – had come to give a talk to the senior pupils. But there was something different about today. Even as they were watching, a camera crew turned up, swiftly followed by two large men wearing dark suits and sunglasses who looked around shiftily as if they were secret-service agents in a bad American spy movie.

"*He* doesn't look like someone from the press," said Eel, pointing at one of the men in dark glasses. He saw her and scowled, then turned his back and eyed a group of Swan pupils making their way up the front steps of the school, some already wearing their practice clothes and with ballet shoes slung round their necks. He watched them closely as if he thought that their leotards and leg warmers were very suspicious and clear evidence of criminal intent.

"Maybe they're just pretending to be photographers and they're really undercover police officers investigating a terrible crime!"

said Eel. "That man's moustache looks fake to me; it's exactly like the one Tom wore in *Bugsy Malone* for end-of-term concert." She wriggled excitedly at the thought, showing just how she'd got her nickname.

"Why would the police want to stake out a stage school?" asked Aeysha reasonably.

"For crimes against art?" said Tom with a grin. "Maybe someone reported your performance in the end-of-term concert to *Crimestoppers*, Eel. You're probably about to be arrested for murdering pirouettes."

Eel looked so indignant that everyone laughed.

"Only joking, Eel," said Tom hurriedly. "You're a brilliant dancer. The best."

"I'm not quite the best," said Eel. "Not yet, anyway. But one day I will be, if I keep practising." She knew that talent wasn't enough; if she was going to be a great dancer she had to work her socks off, and then she would need some luck too.

"Well, I think we ought to tell Miss Swan about the photographers," said Georgia.

"She already knows," came a quiet voice. Everyone swung round to look at Olivia

3

Marvell, who was balanced on one foot on the high-wire suspended across the studio. She was reflected back at them several times in the huge mirrors hung on the wall. Unfazed by her friends' attention, she coolly performed a perfect somersault to dismount. As she untied her long dark hair, a gentle smile twitched around the corners of her mouth and her eyes sparkled, giving her serious face a luminous quality as if it was lit from within.

"Liv Marvell, you've been keeping secrets from your best friends, and you know that's not allowed," said Tom accusingly.

"*And* from your little sister. It's an outrage," said Eel with a little jiggle. Olivia looked guilty; she felt really torn. She longed to tell them everything she'd discovered that morning. She'd overheard her grandmother, Alicia Swan, talking on her mobile to the theatre director Jon James. He'd recently had a big hit on the West End stage with a revival of *The Sound of Music*, featuring several Swan children, including Tom and Georgia. It was clear from what Olivia had heard that Jon was planning a new production of a very famous play with all-star Hollywood casting. But she had promised Gran that she wouldn't say a word until Alicia herself had made an announcement at the traditional start-of-term assembly.

Olivia and Eel were the granddaughters of Alicia Swan, a former star of the West End stage who owned the Swan Academy. They lived with her on the top floor of the stage school while their dad, Jack, a famous high-wire walker, travelled the world trying to restore the Marvell family fortunes. He was currently finishing making a documentary in Snake Canyon in Idaho.

Olivia felt really tempted to spill the beans. After all, everyone would soon know why the photographers and bodyguards were outside so did it really matter if she told her friends a few minutes early? It could do no harm, surely. But she didn't want to break Alicia's trust. Alicia hadn't been looking well recently and Olivia, whose relationship with her grandmother had sometimes been prickly, felt protective towards her. Alicia was a beautiful woman but her eyes had the hollowed contours of someone who wasn't sleeping well and she was jumpy too. She was getting an awful lot of calls, some on her mobile like the one Olivia had overheard this morning, but the landline was unusually busy as well. Only that morning at breakfast the house phone had rung and rung. Alicia hadn't answered it but just kept looking at it as if it was about to bite her. When Eel, fed up with the noise, had gone to pick it up Alicia had snapped at her granddaughter with a sharpness that wasn't like her.

Alicia had then gone into the living room to take the call, closing the door firmly behind her. "Gran's behaving very oddly," Eel had hissed to her sister. "And it's not the first time she's almost bitten my head off. Do you think we should tell Dad?"

Olivia bit her lip. "I'm worried about her too but I don't think we should bother Jack. He's busy trying to finish his film. And anyway, he should be back quite soon." She sighed. "I wish he was here. I do miss him. Gran's just not been herself since she heard about the building next door. It's as if she's still Gran, but a paler, more irritable version."

At the end of last term, after flying to America to act in a movie and provide coaching for its two young American stars, Cosmo and Cosima Wood, Alicia had finally raised enough money to buy the derelict building next door to the Swan. She had long dreamed of expanding the school. She had expected to be the only bidder for the building, which was owned by the council and had been lying empty for years, but at the last minute somebody else had unexpectedly put in a higher sealed bid. Olivia and Eel had been there when the bad news had come through and seen Alicia crumple like an elegant old house whose foundations had suddenly been removed. She had set her heart on the Swan's expansion. She wanted so many more children to be able to benefit from its training, which was recognized as the best in the country, and also to set up weekend and after-school courses for children who couldn't attend the Swan full time.

Staring at her friends' expectant faces, Olivia decided she couldn't betray her gran's confidence, even though it was very tempting. And anyway, it made her feel quite tingly and powerful to know something that no one else did, and which everyone was desperate to find out about.

"Please tell us, Livy. We promise not to tell," said Georgia, her cheeks pink with excitement making her look more like a pretty china doll than ever.

"I am sorry but I really can't," said Olivia. "All I can tell you is that it's connected to her trip to Hollywood last term. I only found out myself this morning when I heard her talking on her mobile."

"Oh, come on, Livy!" cried Aeysha. "Who was Miss Swan talking to?"

"My lips are super-glued shut," grinned Olivia.

"You can't do this to us, Liv," groaned Tom.

"We could tickle her to extract the information. It's what I always do to make Livy tell me things," suggested Eel seriously. "She's got very ticklish feet."

But Olivia was saved by the school bell. It was the first day of the summer term at the Swan Academy and like every term it would begin with assembly in the school hall, followed by vocational lessons. Soon the entire academy would reverberate to the sound of singing and dancing and acting classes.

"I'm bursting to tell you, but you'll just have to be patient," said Olivia as she started to put away the wire. "All will be revealed in just a few minutes. I promised Gran that I wouldn't let the cat out of the bag, and a promise is a promise. I can't break it."

"What cat?" asked Eel. "I didn't know we had a cat." Everyone laughed, and Olivia looked hard at her smart little sister. It wasn't always easy to tell if she was playing the fool or not.

"There is no cat, Eel. But there is an invitation to tea for all of you after lessons this afternoon. Gran asked me to ask you," said Olivia. Her eyes gleamed mischievously. "There'll be chocolate cake and surprise guests, who I think you'll want to meet." Tom, Georgia and Aeysha looked at each other excitedly and that moment the bell rang again.

"Oh no, I've left my score for *Les Miserables* up in the flat and I need it for Singing first period," said Olivia, rifling through her bag. "I'll meet you all in the hall." She left the others and took the stairs two at a time as she ran towards the flat. She gave a little skip and put her worries about Alicia out of her mind; she was really looking forward to the summer term at the Swan.

Chapter Two

The voice at the other end of the phone was smooth. "If you know what's good for you," it said, "you'll accept our offer for the school. Otherwise, Miss Swan, we might have to use a little persuasion, and that won't be nice for you or your pupils."

"Are you threatening me?" said Alicia with a steely note in her voice. "I'll go to the police. They'll soon put an end to your bullying. There are laws against this kind of intimidation."

"Oh, I wouldn't advise that," said the voice silkily. "All those little dancers and their precious little legs. You wouldn't want anything to happen to them, would you? However would you live with yourself?" There was a tiny pause and then the voice added, "I hear your own granddaughter is a very, very talented dancer. It would be such a pity if she or her sister had some kind of accident. . ."

The voice trailed off. Alicia slammed the phone down. She was very pale and her hands were shaking. She stood up and turned around. She gasped when she saw Olivia standing staring at her, the score for the children's version of *Les Miserables* in her trembling hand.

"Gran," whispered Olivia. "Something terrible's happening, isn't it? What's going on?"

Alicia went over and hugged her. As she held Olivia in her arms she thought how she would do anything she could to protect her precious granddaughters. They'd barely had a chance to know their own mother, Toni, who'd died in a plane crash when Olivia and Eel were very young. Alicia glanced at the huge portrait of her daughter on the living-room wall and thought how alike Toni and Olivia were: both unaware of their own beauty, loyal, intense and intensely private as if there was some part of themselves that they refused to make readily available to the world. Toni only allowed that part of herself to show on stage and it had been one of the things that had made her a great actress. Alicia suspected that Olivia was the same and would one day be a brilliant actress too. But for the moment Olivia was only really interested in walking the high-wire.

"It's nothing for you to worry about, Livy darling," she said. "Just some silly people who think they can persuade me to sell the Swan. But that's never going to happen, I promise you."

Olivia felt as if she'd been punched in the stomach. The Swan wasn't just her school, it was her home. The only place she'd ever been able to call home after her previous life in a travelling circus. The thought of losing it and all her friends made her feel sick. She felt as if she had already lost so much in her short life.

"If you're being threatened, you should go to the police," said Olivia, hoping to sound strong and grown up but her voice came out all scratchy because she was trying not to cry. Alicia held Olivia even more tightly and felt grateful that her granddaughter hadn't heard the other side of the conversation and the ominous warnings of the man with the sinister, silky voice. Particularly those concerning Eel and Olivia herself.

"Really, Livy, it's not as bad as it sounded.

It's probably just somebody's idea of a nasty joke. If I was really being threatened, of course I'd go to the police," said Alicia. Her voice sounded a little too jaunty even to her. "I'm going to sort it out, believe me, and in the meantime please don't say anything to anyone. I'm trusting you, just as I trusted you this morning." She sighed. "Now, come on, Livy, we must go downstairs for assembly. Everyone will be wondering what's happened to us. And we've got such exciting news to tell them!"

Alicia held out her hand to Olivia, who helped her down the stairs as fast as her grandmother's arthritis would allow. Alicia squeezed her granddaughter's hand: it wasn't the pain in her hands and feet but the voice on the phone that scared her. That and the look of fear in Olivia's dark eyes.

Alicia Swan gazed across the school hall at her pupils, or the Swans as they were affectionately known in the business. They were frequently to be found performing in London's West End theatres. Georgia and Tom were in *The Sound of Music* at the Duke's Theatre, while other pupils were playing in *Les Miserables* at the

13

Queens and *Billy Elliot* at the Victoria Palace. Two Swans were at the Royal Court in a new play by a young woman playwright that had all the critics raving, and William Todd, who was in the same year as Olivia and her friends, had just finished being the doomed Prince Arthur in the RSC revival of Shakespeare's *King John* at the Roundhouse. William, thought Alicia to herself, must have acted his socks off to get the role of the saintly Arthur, because in reality he was a high-spirited little devil who was always playing practical jokes. She shuddered when she remembered the stink bomb incident when he had been in Year Three.

Alicia was proud of all her pupils and they were proud to be Swans – there was fierce competition to get into the school and those who won a place knew that they had been the lucky ones.

"The ducklings, they all look very happy to be back," said Pablo Catalano, the Spanish circus-skills teacher, to one of his colleagues.

"They do indeed," agreed Sebastian Shaw, who was head of acting. "And when they hear Miss Swan's news I predict they're going to be positively ecstatic!"

14

Pablo shrugged. Like Olivia, he didn't really care about celebrities; he just wanted to teach circus to children who really wanted to learn. Olivia was his star pupil, perhaps not surprisingly as she and Eel had grown up in a travelling circus run by their dad, Jack Marvell. Pablo watched as Alicia raised her hand to silence the chattering children. She looked very pale and her voice didn't quite ring with its usual authority.

"Welcome back, everyone," she said. "It's lovely to see you all again and I hope you're all raring to go because it's going to be a very busy term indeed. You're all going to have to work very hard, because we are determined that the Swan is going to remain the country's leading stage school. Of course, there are also public examinations this year for those of you in Year Eleven, and I don't want anyone to say that we neglect the academic side of things at the Swan. We are as proud of our examination results as we are of winning leading roles on stage and in film, TV and advertising campaigns." She looked hard at the Year Eleven pupils. "I'm expecting great things from you and I know that you won't let me down. Last year's Year Eleven

15

gave us our best examination results ever, and I know that you are going to surpass them."

"No pressure then, Miss Swan," called out Kasha Kasparian, one of the most popular boys in Year Eleven. Everyone grinned.

"Believe me, Kasha, exam pressure is a doddle compared with the pressures you'll be facing in the music business," said Alicia drily, but there was a twinkle in her eye. At just sixteen, Kasha already had a recording contract and looked set for stardom but his headmistress had successfully persuaded him to stay on at school, arguing that fame could be fickle. "And you never know, Kasha," she'd said, "you might decide you want to be a brain surgeon one day. You're bright enough. Take your exams and keep all your options open." Alicia was pleased that Kasha had taken her advice; even though she was confident that he had a dazzling future ahead as a singer-songwriter. But nothing was ever guaranteed in this business. There were plenty who became stars in their teens and who were burned out by the time they were twenty and on the scrapheap. Show business could be so cruel.

"Now," said Alicia briskly, although her

voice shook a little. "As I'm sure many of you have already heard, sadly we were unsuccessful in our bid to buy the derelict building next door. I won't deny that I'm disappointed, as it would have been a wonderful opportunity to expand the school. I don't know who has bought the land or what they're planning to do with it, but there has been no demolition or building work so far. I just hope that when they do start it won't prove too disruptive to our work here, which will, of course, continue as usual. I'm sure I don't need to tell any of you this, but you are not to go anywhere near the building site. Such places can be very dangerous, so I want you all to promise me to keep away. I don't want any accidents." Alicia gave a little shudder.

Then, using all her acting skills, she broke into a huge smile. "Now, I have some other news that I think you will all find far more fascinating. Some of you may have read rumours on the Internet and in the media that a big new production of *Peter Pan* is being planned for the West End this summer, one using child professionals rather than adult actors in the main roles. Well, I'm delighted to be able to tell you that the rumours are true and everything will be announced at a press conference tomorrow morning." A little buzz of excitement passed around the hall. "The good news is that this is a real opportunity for those of you who hope to work this term and who don't already have contracts in other shows. As soon as I hear about audition dates I'll let you know, but they could be as early as next week. The bad news is that the roles of Peter Pan and Wendy have already been cast." A groan went up from some parts of the hall. Alicia looked at everyone and her eyes were sparkling. She continued, "But as this is turning into one of those good news/bad news assemblies, the good news is that the roles have gone to Swan children."

The children looked at each other, puzzled. Who could it be? Normally everybody knew when someone was trying out for a role. That kind of secret just couldn't be kept at the Swan, and in any case, Alicia always insisted on total transparency when it came to auditions so that Swan pupils could be supportive of each other rather than seeing each other as rivals. Alicia clapped her hands and everyone fell silent again.

"Later today we will have two brand-new pupils starting at the Swan and they will be staying with us for as long as they are rehearsing and appearing in *Peter Pan*. I'm sure that you will all do your best to make them feel welcome here."

"Oh, Miss Swan, you're killing us!" called William Todd. "Don't keep us in suspense. Who is it?"

Alicia smiled. "I was just coming to that." Ever the actress, she paused for such a long time the listening children thought they might burst, and then said, "Our newest Swan pupils are two people whose names I know will be familiar to you all: Cosmo and Cosima Wood."

The room exploded into gasps and cheers. Everybody had heard of Cosmo and Cosima Wood, the twelve-year-old American twins who were the youngest of a distinguished American acting dynasty even more famous than the Barrymores or the Redgraves. Members of the Wood family had been appearing on stage without skipping a generation since the early nineteenth century.

Cosmo and Cosima had been performing almost since the day they were born. They had their own TV series and their own clothing range and they often appeared in the pages of the gossip magazines, frequently dressed in his'n'her versions of the same outfit. They had lived their entire lives in the spotlight: their father, Jasper Wood, had been on stage playing Hamlet at the Lincoln Center in New York on the night his wife, the famous actress Melissa Drew, gave birth to the twins. At the curtain call he had stepped forward, quietened the rapturous applause and announced the news by declaring, "Tonight there are two new additions to the Wood family business: a brilliant actor and actress have been born." Jasper and Melissa had divorced a few months later but the twins had stayed in the US with their dad after their mother gave up acting and moved to Greece to marry a shipping heir. She'd quickly had more children and had almost no contact with Cosmo and Cosima, although she had once referred to them in an interview with a Greek newspaper as "my lost babies".

Alicia let the children talk for a few more seconds before clapping her hands for silence. "I have every confidence that you will all treat Cosmo and Cosima as you would any fellow professional and make their stay here in London as happy as possible, and their time at the Swan a memorable one," she said, looking at her watch. "Please go to your first lessons of the afternoon. The bell will ring any minute."

The children began to move out of the hall still talking animatedly to each other. They were used to rubbing shoulders with famous people: the Swan already boasted the offspring of several celebrities as pupils, and it had produced more than its fair share of stars. But the Swan had never had anyone quite as famous as the Wood twins before.

"So that explains all the photographers hanging around outside," said Tom.

"And those men in suits really are bodyguards like you see in the movies!" added Aeysha.

Olivia nodded. "I really did want to tell you all but I'd given my word to Gran that I wouldn't. But you will all come to tea after school to meet Cosmo and Cosima, won't you? They're going to be in our class. They're going to be doing some work with Gran and Mr Shaw this afternoon, but Gran wants to make sure that they recognise some friendly faces when they arrive after the press conference tomorrow."

"I wouldn't miss it for anything," said

Aeysha before she rushed away to her jazz class.

"Cake and the Wood twins, that's not an invite anyone could turn down! I wonder which will be nicer?" said Tom, walking towards singing in the Callas Room with Olivia. He noticed his friend's pale, closed face. "Is everything all right, Liv?" he asked. "You look a bit glum."

Before Olivia could answer, the bell sounded loudly. It was as though it was some kind of cue, because the second it died away there was a huge roar of noise from the building site next door, with lots of banging and the high-pitched squeal and shudder of drills. It sounded as if somebody had turned on all the machinery at once. Olivia and Tom stared at each other. It felt as if the Swan was suddenly at the centre of an angry, deafening thunderstorm.

Chapter Three

Cosmo and Cosima Wood stood in the middle of the Judi Dench rehearsal room on the first floor of the Swan. They were playing Wendy and Peter in a scene from *Peter Pan*, watched closely by Alicia and Sebastian Shaw.

"Peter, how old are you?" asked Cosima, sounding as if she had absolutely no interest in the answer.

"I don't know, but quite young, Wendy," replied Cosmo with a strange transatlantic twang that made him sound half Californian and half Cockney, a bit like Dick Van Dyke in *Mary Poppins*. "I ran away the day I was born."

"Ran away? Why?" asked Cosima, raising her arms stiffly on the word "why" as if she was trying to round up a herd of particularly stubborn cows. Alicia could feel Sebastian glance her way. She resisted meeting his eye: she knew exactly what he was thinking, and it wasn't encouraging. "Why?" hissed Cosima again, more loudly this time.

"Because I heard Father and Mother talking of what I was to be when I became a man. I want always to be a little boy and have fun. . ." Cosmo's next few words were drowned out by a terrible racket from the building site next door. The floor of the rehearsal room trembled slightly as if it was complaining.

Cosmo broke off and raised his eyes to the heavens. "They warned me that conditions in West End theatre were primitive," he drawled, "but nobody told me that I'd be trying to act on a demolition site." He looked at his sister and added nastily: "It's tough enough having to act with someone like Cosi who demolishes the meaning of the text at every opportunity."

"Zip it, Cosmo. Nobody cares what you think," his sister replied.

"Children, children. . ." began Alicia, but she got no further because the terrible noise started up again.

Almost immediately the door flew open

and Pablo appeared in the doorway, his eyes flashing. "This is impossible! This noise has scrambled my brain. My poor little ducklings, they shake like leaves in a big storm when they are on the wire. We cannot work in these conditions. Miss Alicia, I beg of you, please stop this noise! It is monstrous."

Alicia sighed. "I'll go and talk to whoever is running the site," she said wearily. "Please take Cosmo and Cosima up to my flat, Sebastian. It's almost time for the final afternoon bell anyway. Olivia and Eel and their friends will be coming up for tea shortly. Would you mind putting the kettle on?"

As she turned to go, Cosima blurted out loudly, "I can't do this. I can't play Wendy on stage. I just can't do it. I've told Dad but he just bawls me out. Why won't someone listen?"

Alicia turned back. Cosmo raised his eyes to the heavens and said, "Oh no, here we go again, the princess is whining. Cut it out, Cosi. Dad and I are fed up with your moaning twenty-four seven."

Alicia frowned at him before turning to Cosima. "Of course you'll be able to play Wendy," she said kindly. "I'm going to make sure that you will. That's my job. You just need more self-belief, Cosi. You're going to be fine."

Cosima said nothing, but she shook her head sadly.

"Jeez, yes," said Cosmo. "She's going to be just awesome. I don't think."

"Cosmo!" said Alicia warningly and there was something in her tone that made him stop, and even look a little bashful.

"Sorry," he muttered, popping a wad of gum into his mouth. She opened the door of the rehearsal room and found her way blocked by the two man-mountains that were the twins' minders. They eyed her with suspicion before stepping aside reluctantly.

Alicia set off downstairs. The noise was deafening and all classes seemed to have ended prematurely. She felt as if she was centuries old. Normally she loved the first day of term, but it had been a very stressful afternoon. For a start, there had been the threatening phone call, with the anonymous voice at the end of the line trying to persuade her yet again to sell the Swan for a ludicrously knock-down price. Today's call had been the most menacing yet. The sensible thing would be to go straight to the police but

26

there was something about the caller's voice that made Alicia feel frightened. She was certain he would have no hesitation in carrying out his threats.

It had certainly been a most exhausting day. Getting the Wood twins into the building via the river entrance to avoid the photographers had proved difficult enough, and made Alicia realise that having them at the Swan might prove more disruptive than she'd imagined. She just hoped that after the press conference tomorrow morning, where the details of the production and its casting would be announced, that interest would dissipate and the photographers would decamp elsewhere. The twins' minders were another problem she hadn't anticipated. It was like having two human Rottweilers on the premises. Some of the younger children were quite scared of them. Alicia wondered whether they could be persuaded to smile occasionally and at least take off their sunglasses when they were inside the Swan.

But she had far more pressing things to worry about than the twins' minders: seeing Cosmo and Cosima act was a sharp reminder of what a long, hard job it would be to get them ready for their West End debut. Despite what she'd said to Cosima, she wasn't convinced that they'd ever be truly ready.

And they certainly wouldn't be if this dreadful noise kept up. Alicia felt as if she'd been spun around in a concrete mixer all afternoon. There could be months of disruption ahead from the building site next door. She had to deal with it and find a way to limit it. She just hoped that whoever had bought the building would be reasonable and willing to discuss the situation with her. Then, as she reached the front door of the Swan, the noise suddenly stopped.

The silence was exquisite for a few seconds and then it was filled by the clang of the bell marking the end of the Swan school day. She waited for a moment, expecting the building site noise to resume again but all was silence except for the chirp of a blackbird and the sound of two hundred and fifty children heading home. Alicia turned on her heel and started to climb the stairs towards the flat. Maybe that was the end of the disruption? If it happened again tomorrow she'd respond, but her nerves were too stretched for any further confrontation today.

Chapter Four

The tea party in Alicia's flat was not going well. In fact, thought Olivia, it was a disaster, unfolding like a slow-motion car crash before her eyes. She kept looking at the clock in the hope they'd get through to the end without anyone getting seriously hurt. Cosmo and Cosima seemed to have had some kind of argument and kept glaring at each other, and the Swans found themselves unexpectedly shy when faced with the famous Hollywood twins. Tom, who was normally so sunny and funny, was stiff and formal, and Georgia and Aeysha were unusually subdued.

Only Eel was her usual self, prattling on about dancing and asking Cosmo about his favourite ballet, a question that Cosmo didn't even deign to acknowledge, let alone answer. He refused all food and just chewed gum noisily all the way through tea. He kept texting and checking his iPhone, which the others thought was very rude. Cosima sat looking miserable, eyes downcast, nibbling on the corner of a sandwich. She reminded Olivia of a nervous and very pretty squirrel.

It was made worse because while Alicia and Sebastian had tactfully withdrawn to give the children a chance to get to know each other, the twins' minders stood in the corner glowering and looking suspiciously around as if they were convinced that the tea party wasn't a tea party at all but a dastardly plot to kidnap the twins and hold them for ransom. Not surprisingly, the conversation was somewhat stilted. Questions about whether the twins had any pets, had read all the *Harry Potter* novels or had been to England before were greeted with a monosyllabic grunt from Cosmo or an unhappy little shake of the head from Cosima. At one point, when Georgia started enthusing about *Peter Pan*, saying how much she loved the story about the boy who refused to grow up and how she wished she wasn't a girl so she could play one of the Lost

Boys, Cosmo yawned very loudly and started to play a game on his phone. Georgia had looked really hurt and flushed very pink, while Olivia felt furious on her behalf.

In their TV series in which they supposedly played a version of themselves, Cosmo and Cosima came across as a pair of cool, quick-witted pranksters who never stopped joking and kidding around. In real life they barely said a word. Olivia wondered if it was because they didn't have a script to follow. There seemed to be a vast chasm between the real Wood twins and their celebrity image.

After a while Olivia and the others began to talk amongst themselves to fill in the silences. Out of the corner of her eye, Olivia could see Cosima visibly relax. She wondered whether Cosima might be quite nice away from her ghastly brother.

Aeysha started to talk about her holidays. "Mum says we might be able to go to Disney World in Florida next summer!" she said excitedly.

"That'd be awesome," said Georgia.

"No, it wouldn't," grunted Cosmo. "Disney World sucks."

31

"How would you know?" asked Tom sharply, seeing Aeysha's face drop.

"We had our tenth birthday party there," replied Cosmo. "They closed the place specially."

"You mean you had the whole of Disney World to yourselves?"

Cosmo puffed out his chest proudly. "Yep," he said. Cosima looked embarrassed.

"They've only ever done it for us," added Cosmo. "It still sucked, though." He took out his gum and stuck it under the table. Olivia made a mental note to remove it later before Alicia discovered it.

"But wasn't it amazing to have Disney World closed specially for you?" said Georgia. "It must have made you feel really special."

"We *are* special," drawled Cosmo flatly, as if Georgia were a bit slow. Cosima looked as if she wanted the floor to open up and the others just looked at each other, embarrassed.

Eel broke the silence. "How many auditions did you have before you got cast as Peter Pan and Wendy?" she asked very sweetly.

"Auditions?" said Cosmo, looking astounded. "We've never had to audition for anything in our lives. We're not like you kids.

We were in a movie when we were six weeks old. We played the baby and Angelina Jolie was our mom. We were voted cutest newcomers by the biggest Hollywood fan site. We've had loads of awards since. We pick and choose from stuff we're offered. Auditions! They're for losers."

"Oh," said Eel, surprised. "So how do you know if you're any good? You could just be getting roles because of who you are, not because you've got any talent."

Olivia kicked Eel's ankle very hard under the table, while Georgia's apple juice went down the wrong way and Tom had to thump her hard on the back. Cosmo looked at Eel as if she had just crawled out from beneath a stone and Cosima seemed to be looking frantically for the nearest exit. Her cheeks were flaming. Aeysha quickly thrust a plate under Cosmo's nose and said a little too brightly, "Chocolate cake?"

"You're kidding?" drawled Cosmo. "I'm wheat- and dairy-free."

"Don't forget charm-free," muttered Cosima.

Her brother glared at her. "Least I'm not talent-free," he snarled.

"Oh yeah?" snapped Cosima. Cosmo

flushed. Olivia thought they looked like tigers ready to spring at each other.

Aeysha coughed. "Where are you living while you're in London?" she asked.

"We have a suite at the Savoy Hotel," said Cosmo. "It sucks."

"No, it doesn't, Cosmo," said Cosima sharply. "It's totally neat." She looked a little wistful. "But I wish we could live in a real apartment like this and be just like other kids."

Cosmo made a braying sound, like a donkey laughing. "But we're not like other kids, Cosi. We're the Wood twins and don't you forget it."

"As if," sighed Cosima.

At that moment, Alicia and Sebastian came back. "Why don't you show the twins round the Swan?" said Alicia. Cosmo looked totally underwhelmed at the idea but Alicia was insistent. She explained that the Swan was a bit of a warren and a tour would make everything much easier for them when they started the next day. The children set off, with Cosmo trailing behind still playing a game on his phone. The minders followed at a distance.

* * * * *

Alicia and Sebastian watched them go.

"This isn't going to be easy, Alicia," said Sebastian.

"No," said Alicia. "In fact, it's going to be much harder than I thought. I'm really worried about the twins, Seb. You saw them acting this afternoon. I know it's still early days but they're going to be so exposed on the West End stage. When I was doing the film with them in Hollywood I strongly advised Jasper Wood against doing *Peter Pan* but he still went ahead and signed the contract on their behalf. They may be rich and famous the world over but they're still just a couple of twelve-year-old kids and I can't bear to think of them being sacrificed on the altar of the Wood family ambitions."

"I can see why Jasper Wood was keen," replied Sebastian. "I know he's still a big star but his career is rumoured to be on the skids. His last couple of movies flopped and he hasn't been on Broadway for years. Presumably he wants to make sure that his kids carry on the family name. But I'm curious. Why did you agree to this? Why get involved in something so risky?"

"How could I say no?" said Alicia. "I

think I genuinely helped them improve their performances in the film, and the editing will do the rest. Once Jasper had made up his mind that the twins were going to do *Peter Pan*, I felt I had to do anything I could to prevent a catastrophe. They've never even been on stage before, poor little mites."

"I don't think that Cosmo qualifies as a poor little mite; more of a spoiled little brat," said Sebastian drily.

Alicia nodded. "I don't think he'll be half so cocky when he realises the challenge he's up against. I just hope that the rest of the principals in the cast go all out to help them."

"Who's playing Captain Hook?" asked Sebastian.

"I imagine they'll double Mr Darling and Captain Hook, but Jon wouldn't tell me who the actor is. It's top secret, so it must be a huge name. Even the twins don't know who it is. There's more security round this show than there is around the Crown Jewels. Everyone involved has had to sign confidentiality agreements, and I had to get special permission just to announce it at assembly this afternoon. I just hope Captain Hook is played by someone who'll be generous and supportive towards the twins." Alicia shook her head gravely. "I'm seriously worried their West End debut is going to backfire and that'll end up reflecting badly on the Swan too. But there's no going back now. We'll just have to make the best of a bad situation and hope that the critics don't eat them up and spit them out." She looked at her watch. "I'd better call Tom and Georgia. Their taxi will be here any moment to take them to the Duke's for *The Sound of Music*." She cocked her head to one side, reminding Sebastian of a delicate bird. "Isn't this lack of building-site noise bliss?"

Everyone rushed off about their business and suddenly Olivia found herself alone with the twins and their minders while they waited for their limo to arrive to take them back to their hotel. Cosmo was still playing on his phone.

Olivia and Cosima looked at each other awkwardly. Olivia was itching to get away too. She had had quite enough of the Wood twins for one day. She thought Cosmo was one of the most unpleasant boys she had ever met. There was something about his pampered arrogance that reminded her of Katie Wilkes-Cox, a former

Swan pupil who had hated Olivia and done everything she could to hurt her. As for Cosima, Olivia found her self-pity and lack of spark and animation depressing; she seemed to come alive only when she was arguing with her brother. In many ways, she was just as self-absorbed.

"Do you like it here at the Swan?" asked Cosima shyly.

Olivia realised that it was the first question either of the twins had asked; throughout tea they had let the Swans do all the questioning and shown no interest in anybody else's lives. She nodded. "Yes," she said. "Though I hated it when I first came here two terms ago. I loathed all the acting and singing and particularly the dancing, but now I love it. I wouldn't want to be anywhere else. Well, I still don't like dancing much, but I don't do very much of that. I do circus instead. High-wire and trapeze mostly."

"You can walk the high-wire?" said Cosima. "Oh my gosh! That's totally awesome."

"Yes," said Olivia. "I used to live in a travelling circus with my dad, Jack Marvell. He's a high-wire walker."

"Your dad's the Great Marvello? Wow! I've seen clips of him on YouTube walking across

Niagara Falls. You have the coolest dad on the planet. I'd love to meet him."

Olivia was delighted by Cosima's words. "He's away in the US making a documentary but he's promised to come home very soon," she said. "Eel and I really miss him. I just wish he could get a job here in London for a while." She smiled at Cosima. "You could learn the high-wire while you're at the Swan."

Cosima looked worried. "Er, well, I'm not good at heights."

"Oh, you can start just a few centimetres off the ground."

Cosima still looked worried. "I guess my dad wouldn't like it," she muttered.

"No, he wouldn't, because it's just circus garbage," said Cosmo, looking up from his phone for a millisecond. "Move it, Cosi, the limo's here. Dad's texted me – he's just touched down at Heathrow and he's going straight to the hotel. He wants to talk to us about the press conference tomorrow."

He stalked away without even saying goodbye. Olivia felt furious. Cosima smiled apologetically and followed him meekly, sighing heavily. Olivia watched her go. She thought how many girls envied Cosima Wood and fantasised about what it must be like to be her, but from what Olivia had seen, it was a real downer. Well, she wasn't going to waste any more time on the Wood twins. She doubted that she'd have much to do with them. Cosmo clearly thought that everyone at the Swan was beneath him, and she couldn't imagine that she and Cosi would ever be friends in the same way she was with Georgia, Aeysha and Tom. She hurried away to find Pablo, who had promised to give her a trapeze lesson.

Chapter Five

Olivia was eating her breakfast when her mobile phone rang.

"Olivia?" said an American voice hesitantly.

"Cosima!" said Olivia, surprised. "How did you get my number?"

"I hope you don't mind. I asked Jon James for it." Cosima paused. "I wanted to ask you a big favour."

"What is it?" asked Olivia cautiously. She really didn't want to get involved with the twins more than was necessary but, for Alicia's sake, she didn't want to be rude either. Having seen how Cosmo and Cosima had behaved at tea last night, she reckoned they wouldn't be greeted with open arms by the rest of the Swan pupils and might have quite a hard time at the school.

41

"I hoped that you would come to the press conference this morning," said Cosima. Then she added shyly, "I guess I'd feel happier if there was a friendly face in the crowd."

"But Cosmo and your dad will be there. And Gran."

"I know," said Cosi firmly. "But I want you to be there too."

Olivia sighed inwardly. Cosima had called it a favour but there was something about her manner that made it sound like an order at the same time. She hoped that Cosima hadn't singled her out to be her special friend while she was at the Swan. But Olivia wanted to be kind, because after all she knew only too well what it was like to be thrust into a strange situation beyond your control. When she and Eel had arrived at the Swan two terms ago, Olivia felt everyone thought they were weird because they'd been in a circus, and being Alicia's granddaughters singled them out too. She thought it must be the same for Cosima and Cosmo but even more so. If you had been famous all your life like the twins had, it must be impossible to make real friends.

"I'll have to ask Gran," said Olivia, hoping

she sounded more enthusiastic than she felt.

"Cool," said Cosima. "I think Jon is calling her now. Catch ya later."

Cosima was right. Alicia was that very minute talking to Jon James on her mobile. Jon was very fond of both the Marvell girls: Eel's impromptu performance as Gretl on press night had saved his production of *The Sound of Music* and turned it into the hit of the season, and he admired Olivia for her extraordinary bravery in saving Katie Wilkes-Cox, another member of the cast, from certain death, even though Katie had been making her life a misery.

"Cosima really does seem very keen for Livy to be there," Jon told Alicia. "And anything that will help put the twins at their ease can only be a good thing." Then he added cryptically, "In fact, there's going to be an announcement that both the Marvell girls will enjoy. You'd better bring Eel too."

Before Alicia could ask him what he meant, Jon moved on. "How was your session with the twins yesterday?" Alicia paused just a fraction too long. "Tell me the truth!" he demanded.

Alicia sighed. "As you well know, Jon," she

said drily, "the truth is a precious commodity and we must use it sparingly. Particularly in the theatre."

Jon laughed. "OK, you've told me everything I need to know. Lots of hard work ahead for all of us, then. I just hope that the casting coup of the century doesn't turn out to be a catastrophe instead. See you in a couple of hours."

Alicia said goodbye and turned to Olivia. "I can see from your face that Cosima's already asked you this – but would you like to come to the press conference?" asked Alicia. She saw the doubt in Olivia's eyes. "I don't want to force you to be friends with Cosima. But I think just at the moment she needs all the support she can get. Jon and I would be very grateful if you would humour her, at least today."

"The problem with the Wood twins is that people humour them all the time," said Olivia. "But I will come, Gran. But more for your sake, and for Jon's, not for Cosima's."

"Thank you, Livy. It's kind of you. You can go to your first two lessons and then meet me in the foyer at ten o'clock. And Jon wants Eel to be there too. Do you want to tell her or shall I?"

"I'll find her," said Olivia, gathering up her homework books. She knew that her little sister would be thrilled to be going to the press conference. Unlike Olivia, who shrank away from the bright lights, Eel loved the glamour of show business.

"It's going to be a packed day," said Alicia. "But, and thank heavens for small mercies, at least there's no repeat of yesterday's dreadful noise." Olivia headed off downstairs to find Eel, who was doing a before-school class in the Pavlova dance studio. As she got to the door, the bell for first lessons rang. The second it stopped, the machines on the building site next door started up in a great cacophony of noise.

Two hours later, Alicia, Olivia and Eel were sitting in the front row of the Imperial Theatre. Behind them, the gathered press were getting restless. They had already been introduced to Jon James and the production's designer, Lucy Parks-Davies, whose collapsing set for the National Theatre's *A Midsummer Night's Dream* had won her every award going. The choreographer was Tippi Leone, who famously had been sacked from a TV dance show for saying

45

that one of the celebrity contestants looked like a sack of potatoes with all the dancing skills of a tub of lard and then refusing to withdraw her comments. They had also been introduced to Chloe Bonar, who was playing Mrs Darling, and to the rising young comedian Ric Nighthall, who was going to play Nana the dog. He had been in full furry costume and had raised a few laughs with his antics. They'd even got to see the computer-operated mechanical crocodile with the ticking clock inside its tummy that would pursue Captain Hook. Eel thought it would be rather fun to operate the crocodile. She hoped Jon James would let her have a go.

But everyone was impatient to get to the real meat of the press conference. Since the Wood twins has been spotted arriving at Heathrow forty-eight hours ago, the press had been awash with speculation that they were in London to star as Peter and Wendy, and they were dying to interrogate the most famous twelve-year-olds in the world. But they were also agog to discover who was playing Captain Hook. Seldom had a production so successfully staged-managed its own publicity.

Jon James was talking again, explaining that

the production would be using an innovative new system of flying that would allow the children to soar right out into the auditorium and over the heads of the audience. The camera crew, standing in the aisle next to Olivia and Eel, yawned. Normally they'd have found this interesting but they knew that what their news desks really wanted was good footage of the Wood twins and an interview with whoever was playing Captain Hook. But Olivia was fascinated. She thought she'd very much like to have a go at flying. It sounded fun. She reckoned that her circus skills would stand her in good stead. It crossed her mind that Cosima had said she didn't like heights. How would she cope with flying?

"And now for a real coup," said Jon. "I'd like to introduce you to our flying consultant . . . the one and only Jack Marvell." A cheer erupted from the auditorium. Olivia, Eel and Alicia gasped and Olivia turned to her grandmother accusingly.

"I didn't know, Livy," protested Alicia. "I promise. I'm as astonished as you are. I didn't even know he was back in the country."

Olivia felt really hurt. Even if Jack had

been told to keep his involvement in *Peter Pan* a secret, she thought he ought to have trusted her enough to tell her, or at least let her know that he was back in London. But as soon as she saw him walk on stage, his crumpled clothes and bleary-eyed expression showing he'd just stepped off a plane, her hurt feelings evaporated.

Jack Marvell was a popular and glamorous figure, an old-style hero whose daredevil stunts had long captured the public imagination. He'd made front-page news recently, after his plane had crashed in the Idaho wilds and he'd walked for four days through the wilderness to get help for the injured pilot. The cameramen and the rest of the media had really perked up. This press conference was getting better and better!

When Jack caught sight of Olivia, Eel and Alicia, he gave them a surprised and delighted grin and a thumbs-up. There were a few technical questions and then one of the journalists asked him about the safety of the flying apparatus he would be using.

"It's safer than an aeroplane," said Jack with a confident grin.

"But planes do crash," someone called out.

"Not on their way to Never Land, and

not if I'm the pilot," said Jack firmly. "All the children who fly in this production will be as safe as if their feet had never left the ground. And now, ladies and gentlemen, if you'll excuse me, I've just touched down myself and there are some very important people I have to see." He made his way off stage, through the pass door and down into the auditorium, where he took the seat between Olivia and Eel, squeezed both their hands and whispered, "Hello, girls, I've missed you both so much." Olivia squeezed his hand back very hard and snuggled close to him and Eel got out of her seat and climbed into his lap.

"Dad," whispered Olivia. "Can I have a go at flying?"

"I knew you'd ask me that," said Jack. "I was hoping to sign you up to be my guinea pig. Tom too, if he wants."

On stage, Jon James was back at the microphone. "Now," he said, "this is the moment you've all been waiting for! It gives me enormous pleasure to introduce our Peter and Wendy. Ladies and gentlemen, please put your hands together for Cosmo and Cosima Wood." Some stirring music struck up, composed by the man who would be composing all the music for the show, and Cosmo and Cosima stepped on to the stage into a huge spotlight. Camera shutters clicked. The twins waved and smiled. They looked very shiny, thought Olivia. As if somebody had polished them all over. She could see that Cosmo was holding Cosima's hand very hard and Cosima's smile was unnaturally bright as if she was acting happiness and excitement rather than actually experiencing it. She suddenly caught sight of Olivia and flashed her a grateful smile, full of genuine warmth.

"Now, I know that you are very eager to talk to Cosmo and Cosima, and ask them all about playing Peter and Wendy and making their stage debut here in London, but first I want to introduce you to our Captain Hook. We've managed to keep it so secret that nobody, not even Cosmo and Cosima, have known who they will be acting alongside on stage. But I can now reveal to you, in what I'm sure you will all agree is a brilliant piece of casting, that Captain Hook, and of course Mr Darling, will be played by that celebrated star of stage and screen, Jasper Wood."

The auditorium gasped as Jasper Wood

strode on stage. He was a big man with a mass of dark hair and a hawk-like nose that gave a touch of cruelty to his handsome face. While a huge hubbub broke out among the journalists in the auditorium, all eyes turned to Cosmo and Cosima. How would they react to the news that they'd be acting on stage alongside their father? The cameras went crazy as the Wood children and Jasper were ushered towards each other. Jasper Wood clapped Cosmo on the back and caught Cosima in a massive bear hug and held her very tight. Eventually he broke away from her and raised a hand for silence.

"My amazing, talented son, Cosmo, and his beautiful sister, Cosima, and I are delighted and honoured to be making our West End debuts together in J.M. Barrie's famous play. It means so much to us as a family, a family who have drama running through our veins, to be acting in the capital of the theatrical world, London. I know that I speak for all of us when I say that there is no place on earth we'd rather be, except in Never Land, and I hope that you will accept the invitation to fly there with us and experience its magic." Jasper's ultra-sincere manner and his clearly rehearsed words made Olivia's toes curl. She glanced at Cosima. She looked stiff with shock.

"Twins, how does it feel to know that you'll be acting alongside your dad?" asked a reporter.

"Awesome," said Cosmo. "Just awesome. I know he's going to help us so much. He's the best." Jasper gave a blindingly white smile.

"Cosima, do you think your dad will make a great Captain Hook?" There was a little pause. Then Cosima looked at her dad, smiled very sweetly and said very clearly, "Why, it's perfect casting. He'll hardly need to do any acting at all."

For a split second no one seemed to know quite what to make of this remark but then Jasper Wood slapped his thigh exaggeratedly and said, "My daughter! She's such a comedian. She cracks me up every time." Everyone laughed, but to Olivia it looked as if Cosima was holding back tears.

The journalists were all firing questions and Jasper Wood was fielding them in his big booming voice. Olivia's phone gave a little bleep in her pocket and she pulled it out, glad of the distraction. To her surprise, she saw she had a message from Katie Wilkes-Cox. Olivia hadn't heard from Katie since the afternoon at the Duke's Theatre when she'd come to pick up her things from her dressing room before leaving *The Sound of Music* in disgrace. Pale and subdued, she had thanked Olivia and Tom for saving her life and apologised for having tried to destroy their friendship. Olivia had never expected to hear from her again. She read the message.

> *Hello, Olivia. After everything that happened I expect you're surprised that I'm getting in touch. But this is important. I've got some info that will really interest you. Please call me asap. Katie Wilkes-Cox.*

Olivia read the message again. She was intrigued but also wary. What did Katie want? Time and time again Katie had proved herself untrustworthy, and although she had seemed genuinely sorry for everything she had done, Olivia knew that she should be cautious. Eel leaned over and glanced at the screen.

"Oi," said Olivia affectionately. "Stop reading my private messages."

Eel squeezed her sister's hand. "Don't even think of answering it, Livy. Delete it," she warned. "You know what Katie's like. She's a spider who spins a web. Don't get caught up in it."

Olivia hesitated for a moment. She really wanted to believe that Katie had changed. She had seemed so contrite and broken last time she had seen her. But she'd been fooled by Katie before and got badly hurt because of it. She *was* curious, though. What information could Katie possibly have that would be of interest to her? She hesitated for a second, then pressed the delete button.

Chapter Six

"Breathe in . . . and count to three in your head," said Miss Hanbury. "Hold it, then breathe out, and really try to feel it in your diaphragm."

Olivia and the rest of her class were upstairs in the small rehearsal room having a voice lesson. Olivia enjoyed voice lessons and found them quite soothing, or she did when there wasn't a terrible racket coming from the building site next door. She liked the way that the classes made her think hard about breathing, something that most of the time she did without thinking at all. It was the same when she was on the wire or the trapeze: she was suddenly intensely aware of every muscle in her body. She knew it was the same for Eel when she was dancing: the wonderful sense of being in total control and completely in tune with your body.

"Again," said Miss Hanbury. "One . . . two . . . three . . . hold. . ."

"This is dumb," came a loud American voice from the back. Everyone opened their eyes and looked at Cosmo. Miss Hanbury, who was softly spoken and easily flustered, flushed. Quite a lot of the Swan pupils grumbled about voice classes, which were never as exciting as dance or acting or improvisation, but everybody knew how important they were. You couldn't expect to be heard at the back of a huge theatre unless you could project your voice, and if you were going to take on a role that involved speaking for several hours a night, six nights a week with a matinée thrown in for good measure, you had to know how to use your voice properly or you would damage it very quickly. Cosmo had slid down the side of the wall and was sat unwrapping a piece of gum. He looked up at all the faces staring at him.

"What are you looking at, losers? This class sucks. Breathing! Everybody knows how to breathe. I don't need lessons in how to do it." He stood up and sauntered out with a swagger, as if he was daring anyone to challenge him. Cosima seemed uncertain what to do, then registered all the puzzled, almost hostile faces, and scuttled straight after her brother. They could be heard shouting at each other outside in the corridor.

Since their arrival at the Swan, the Wood twins had not made themselves popular. There were two good reasons for this: the first was because they displayed no obvious talent, and if there was one thing that the Swans all admired, it was raw talent and heaps of it. The other was that they were often rude and disruptive. On the first day, two Year Three pupils, Emmy Lovedale and Bola Omayele, had shyly approached Cosmo and asked him for his autograph. He had bawled at them to get out of his way and if they wanted an autograph they should join his fan club.

Cosmo brought his own food to school, strange concoctions that looked as if they belonged in the chemistry lab. Then, in the dining hall their first lunchtime, Cosima's minders had bundled her straight to the front of the lunch queue, upsetting quite a few people. Cosi had looked apologetic and muttered something about "low blood sugar", but pushing in was pushing in. Cosmo then plonked himself down uninvited at the table where Kasha Kasparian and his friends were sitting and proceeded to rubbish all British pop music, declaring that American bands were the only ones worth listening to.

The voice class wasn't the first lesson that the twins had disrupted either. They were just not used to being at school or being two pupils out of many. They didn't get the concept of putting up your hand before speaking, and just spoke when they felt like it, often over the teachers. They were accustomed to being the sole focus of everyone's attention and didn't like it when they weren't. But the thing that bugged the Swans most was that the twins were just not very good at anything.

Because of this, they were in one of the junior classes for contemporary dance and they hated being in with all the smaller children, some of them as young as eight. In his first lesson, Cosmo had stepped on several pupils' toes and, rather than apologising for his clumsiness, he'd acted as if the children should be grateful to have touched flesh with one of the famous Wood twins.

Olivia, who was no great dancer herself,

had watched aghast as Cosima had completely ignored Miss Taylor's instructions and flung herself across the room straight into the path of two small girls. They'd all ended up in a bruised heap on the floor and, although she was more shocked than hurt, Cosima had decided to scream the place down. Her wailing brought the twins' minders rushing aggressively into the room as if they thought Cosima was being murdered. They had ordered all the children to stand against the wall and treated the two crying eight-year-olds who'd been sent flying by Cosima as if they were a tiny Mafia hit squad. They had withdrawn only when India Taylor had fixed them with her withering gaze and enquired if it was quite normal where they came from for grown men to go round bullying small children.

After that incident, Alicia had insisted that the minders stayed outside the building during school hours, although she had had a row on the phone with Jasper Wood about it. But Alicia had stood her ground and the minders now stood on the school steps, occasionally insisting on searching the Swans' bags as they entered the building.

"They seemed to think that my cheese and tomato baguette might be an offensive weapon," said Aeysha after she'd had her lunchbox inspected and Georgia's jazz shoes were examined minutely by the minders who appeared convinced that they might be hand grenades in disguise.

"It's all so silly!" said Eel, miffed because her before-school dance class had been disrupted while the minders conducted a thorough search of the studio. "They must realise that anyone stupid enough to kidnap the Wood twins would pay millions to give them back again immediately. Imagine spending a moment longer in their company than you had to!"

Her friends had all nodded in agreement, but Olivia said, "Maybe it's not their fault. Maybe it's the way they've been treated and brought up. Gran said that their dad is 'impossible'. He won't listen to her or Jon. I don't think the twins can be very happy. Particularly not Cosima."

"Come on, Liv. Don't tell me you feel sorry for them," said Tom, who was annoyed because Cosima had usurped his seat next to Olivia during morning academic lessons and he had to sit next to Cosmo and listen to his endless moaning.

"Not exactly *sorry*," said Olivia. "They're far too spoiled and privileged for anyone to feel sorry for them but I do know what it's like to feel as if you don't fit in somewhere. It's how I felt when I first came to the Swan."

Suddenly Cosima appeared at her side and started handing out invitations. "Cosmo and I want you all to come to supper tonight at the Savoy to meet my dad," she said.

"Sorry," said Tom quickly, "but Georgie and I have got a *Sound of Music* performance tonight."

"I can't come either," said Aeysha. "I promised my mum I'd help her make a cake for my little brother's birthday, and my Auntie Hema and my cousins are coming over for a game of Monopoly."

Olivia saw Cosi's face and was instantly reminded of a small dog, begging. She felt bad but was relieved that she too had an excuse. "Sorry, nor me," she said. "Eel and I have already arranged to have supper with Jack. We've hardly seen him since he got back. He's been at the Imperial almost day and night getting the flying system in place. But he promised to take us out tonight. I really am sorry."

"Never mind," said Cosima brightly. "I'll tell Dad that we'll have to do it another time."

Chapter Seven

Olivia sat in a large chair in a huge suite in the Savoy. She suddenly felt very small, like Alice after she'd followed the instructions on the bottle labelled "Drink me" in *Alice in Wonderland*. A waiter was opening a bottle of champagne for Jasper Wood. He saw Olivia watching.

"It's the best they have, Octavia," he said in his booming voice that seemed twice as large as it should be, like everything else in the room. "I always say that only the best is worth having. Six hundred pounds a pop and worth every delicious bubble." Olivia goggled as he downed a glass in almost one mouthful. She reckoned that Jasper Wood had just swallowed the fizzy equivalent of a hundred pounds.

Since she'd arrived at the Savoy – in the

limo that had been sent to collect her even though she'd said she would be fine to get the Tube – Olivia had began to appreciate just how different Cosmo and Cosima's lives were from her own or any of the other children at the Swan.

She knew that everyone's circumstances were different: Georgia's mum couldn't afford the fees for the Swan so Georgia wouldn't be able to go if she didn't have a scholarship, and there were lots of other children at the Swan who had bursaries, while others came from families that were comfortably off. Even Katie Wilkes-Cox, who had always been boasting about her mansion and swimming pool, had had to use the sweaty changing rooms and get around on public transport like everyone else. At the Swan you were judged not on how much money you had but on how much talent and how well you used it.

The Wood twins, however, clearly lived in a bubble of luxury and privilege. They didn't have to do a thing for themselves. When Cosmo knocked over his orange juice, he barely seemed to notice. Olivia watched a person who looked suspiciously like an old-fashioned butler rush to mop it up and a waiter immediately handed him a new drink. Meanwhile Jasper's personal assistant was constantly fielding calls. "I'm afraid we can't get that shirt you want back from laundry until tomorrow," he told Jasper apologetically.

Jasper's face darkened. "I want it and I want it now!" he shouted. "Who do they think they're dealing with? I'll pay double, triple if that's what it takes. But get it, and get it now!"

It was like watching an overgrown toddler having a tantrum. Jasper was shouting so loudly that Olivia felt completely embarrassed for him but nobody else seemed to notice. It was obviously considered normal behaviour. Cosmo continued playing on his laptop, only stopping to take a wodge of gum out of his mouth and stick it under a rosewood table, and although she glanced nervously in her dad's direction, Cosi just carried on telling Olivia a long story about a TV movie they had made when they were very little. It had been about two children who had adventures with their dog and Jasper had been furious because the dog was paid more than the twins.

"Yeah, but that was when we were tiny, Cosi," cut in Cosmo. "Before we were really famous. What really upset Dad was that the dog got top billing."

"It was very cute," said Cosi wistfully. "I'd like to have a dog, but it wouldn't be fair on it. I'd never see it. I'm always working."

Jasper was still shouting, "Do you know who I am?" but this time down the phone, and Olivia still felt embarrassed for him.

Olivia thought how strange it must be to live your whole life like this. The Wood family had servants to deal with their every whim but they had no real privacy either. They were constantly surrounded by assistants and minders. Over the Easter holidays Jack had taken his daughters to look round Hampton Court Palace. He'd told them that in the olden days royalty lived their entire lives in semi-public, constantly surrounded by courtiers and servants so that nobody could have an argument or even give birth without everyone hearing and seeing. Olivia thought it must have been horrible to live like that, like being on a stage where the curtain never falls. For Cosi and Cosmo, every day was like a performance with no ending.

Olivia had not expected to find herself at the Savoy that night. She'd been looking forward to spending a rare evening with her dad. Jack always left to work on the flying apparatus for *Peter Pan* long before Olivia and Eel were up in the mornings and wasn't back until after they were asleep in bed. He'd told them it was only for a few weeks. Once the show opened he would have all the time in the world for them and had hinted that he had exciting summer plans for them all. But after Eel had complained that she was the only person in her class who had to make an appointment to see her own dad, and Olivia said that she'd probably spoken to him more when he had been thousands of miles away in Idaho, he had arranged to take them out to supper.

Olivia was worried because when she caught a glimpse of him hurrying out the door one morning, he looked exhausted. He was nearly in as bad a way as Alicia, who was beginning to resemble a walking ghost. Olivia was certain that her gran was still getting threatening phone calls; she'd noticed that Alicia had taken to discreetly unplugging the phone in the evenings. She wanted to talk to Jack about her gran, and check that he wasn't wearing himself out as well.

But just an hour or so after Cosi had invited her to the Savoy, she'd got an apologetic call from Jack saying that he was desperately sorry but he would have to cancel supper tonight. Jon James had told him that the producers wanted to check up on the progress he'd made with the flying equipment, and it was definitely an order not a request, so he couldn't get away. Standing in the corridor between classes while the Swans swirled around her on their way to various rehearsal rooms, Olivia had felt disappointment rise like a lump in her throat.

At that exact same moment Cosi had appeared. "I hear you're free after all, Livy," she said. "So you can come tonight." Olivia had been so astonished she had blurted out, "Yes," and then asked, "How on earth do you know?"

"Oh, my dad just texted me," said Cosi casually. "Jack's needed at the theatre. So it's all worked out perfectly; you'll be able to come to supper after all. It's so neat."

Now, sitting in the Savoy and looking at the way the Wood family operated, Olivia suddenly wondered if Cosi had deliberately manipulated the situation. Perhaps she had got her dad to order Jack to work tonight? Maybe, like Jasper, she was so used to having her own way that she'd do anything to get what she wanted. The thought was so horrible it made Olivia blush just to think it, but she decided not to be too trusting of Cosi and continue to try and keep her at a distance.

Over supper, which had been ordered via room service and came on great silver salvers, Jasper Wood kept up an almost constant monologue about his children's achievements while actually managing to ignore them completely. He had almost finished the bottle of champagne.

"It's like this, Octavia," he said. "The Wood family is different from other families. We're not just a family, we're a family business. We're born into it. It's our destiny. We're theatrical royalty. We're a brand, and as I see it *Peter Pan* is going to extend that brand into a different market. I keep telling the kids, we can make a lot of money out of this if we play it right. It's a business opportunity. Everyone knows that doing theatre in London gives you real credibility. Look at people like that Harry Potter boy, or Keira Knightley. They do the West End so why shouldn't the Woods? I want the twins to do more movies too. Keep the family name on everyone's lips. Did you know they've already got half a million friends on Facebook? That's the way forward, and I've got big plans for them. *Peter Pan* is only the start, Octavia."

"Olivia," said Cosi, embarrassed. "Her name's Olivia."

"Olivia, Octavia, who cares?" boomed Jasper. "It doesn't matter."

"It matters to me," said Olivia quietly. As soon as she said it, she regretted it. She felt Cosi freeze beside her. For a moment, Jasper looked as if he was about to explode, but what he eventually did was even worse. He gave a sarcastic little laugh.

"It may matter to you, but it doesn't matter to anyone else. You're not a name, you're just little Olivia Nobody." The table had suddenly gone very quiet. The waiters stood as if they had been turned to stone. Even Cosmo looked troubled, and Cosi began to sob. Olivia stood up. Her legs were shaking but she was determined not to give Jasper Wood the satisfaction of seeing how much he had hurt her.

"I'm Olivia Marvell," she said with quiet dignity. "Not Olivia Nobody. Thank you for supper but I think I'd better go home now to my family." She hadn't got far down the stairs when she heard Cosi calling her name. For a moment she didn't turn, but there was something so desperate in Cosi's voice that she couldn't bear to ignore her.

"Livy, I'm so sorry. I wish I'd never asked you to come."

"I wish I never had," said Olivia lightly, even though she felt really angry. But she could see that Cosi was distraught.

"Dad hasn't always been like that, you know." Cosi swallowed and tried to explain. "It's only in the last couple of years, since his own career has started to slide. It's as if he's being eaten away inside by disappointment. It all peaked for him around the time Cosmo and I were born and people say he's never been the same since our mom ran away. It's not the money. We've got enough to last us several lifetimes. It's more an obsession with the family name. It's as if he's possessed by it. He says without the Wood name we'd all be nobodies like everyone else." Cosi eyes filled with tears. "But I *want* to be a nobody! I want to live in an ordinary family and make my own way in the world and make my own name for myself. Just like most kids do."

"Have you talked to anyone about all this, Cosi?" asked Olivia, feeling as if she was being sucked into Cosi's life despite herself.

"Only Cosmo, and he doesn't get it. He's bought into the whole 'family business' idea. He thinks it's really cool that he's got all those friends on Facebook. Friends! We don't even update it ourselves. Our PR manager pretends to be us. We haven't got any real friends because we're always on the move or people are too awestruck to really get to know us. It's a real friction between us. I'm scared I'm going to have to be one of the famous Wood twins until I'm old enough to get away and Cosmo's scared that I'm going to quit and his own career will be finished. But it doesn't have to be like that. With some proper training, Cosmo could make it as an actor on his own. In fact, it would be better. We haven't got a hope of moving from child to adult actors together. I only really hold him back, but alone he's got a chance. He has *some* talent, at least." Cosi added fiercely, "I hate my life! The thought of performing on stage in *Peter Pan* makes me feel sick but there's no getting out of it now. Dad would never allow it. Sometimes I think the only thing to do is to run away."

"You could join a circus," said Olivia, trying to lighten the mood a little. She felt so sorry for Cosi. She couldn't imagine what it must be like being made to do something when you hated it as much as Cosi hated being a child star. She knew that if she told Jack she was giving up the high-wire he'd be sad, but he'd respect her decision provided she could show him she'd really thought it through. He wouldn't see it as a betrayal of the Marvell family name. But Cosi didn't have that choice. It was as if Jasper was a thief, stealing Cosi's precious childhood and using it all up until there was nothing left. "Actually, maybe the circus isn't such a good idea if you haven't got a head for heights," added Olivia with a grin.

Cosi gave a smile. "No, you're right, it wouldn't be. I'd be a terrible circus performer just like I'm a terrible actress." She sniffed. "Maybe I'm just terrible. A complete zero."

"Oh, come on, there must be lots of things you're good at," said Olivia.

Cosi shrugged. "I can't think of anything. But there must be some way I can be myself. I'll just have to find out what it is. Would you help me?"

"I guess," said Olivia. She took a deep breath. "Cosi, please don't be angry with me for asking but if we're going to be friends we've got to be honest with each other. Did you get your dad to order my dad to work tonight so I would be free to come to supper?"

Cosi looked appalled. "Of course not, that would be really evil. I'd never do anything like that. . ." Her voice trailed off and she looked stricken. "But of course it's exactly the sort of thing *Jasper* would do. You've seen how he likes to order people around. He must have. . . Oh, Livy, I'm so sorry. You must hate me."

Olivia felt really angry, but she knew it wasn't Cosi's fault.

"Cosi, it's OK, you're not to blame for what your dad does," she said, suddenly feeling enormously tired. "We'll talk tomorrow. I've got to go."

"Livy, you're a real friend." Cosi smiled faintly. "Actually, you're my only friend."

Olivia said goodbye and turned to leave. As she reached the door of the hotel, her phone rang.

"Olivia?" said a voice at the other end. "It's Katie. Katie Wilkes-Cox. We need to meet. There's stuff I have to tell you."

Chapter Eight

"OK, Cosmo and Cosi, you can go now," said Alicia, who could see both twins were looking tired. Particularly Cosima, who was very pale. "You've had a long day." Then she added brightly, "That was much better." She didn't sound convincing even to herself. She felt bone weary.

"No, it wasn't," said Cosima sadly. "We were lousy."

Cosmo opened his mouth to protest.

"OK. Let me rephrase that," said Cosi. "I was lousy and you were slightly less lousy."

"Speak for yourself," said her brother.

"Oh, wake up, Cosmo, and smell the coffee. You've seen some of the Swan kids acting. Even the tinies in Year Three would be better playing

Peter and Wendy than us. They all sing, dance and act much better than we do. We're total amateurs. They've been trained to appear on stage. We've never had any of that. We've just learned the lines, stood about in front of the camera looking cute, picked up what tricks we can as we've gone along and just hoped that because we're the famous Wood twins the director will have been paid handsomely enough to make us look good. Eel's right. How do we know we're any good if we've never had to audition for anything? If we *had* auditioned for *Peter Pan* and been up against any of the Swans, we'd have been shown the door straightaway. Livy doesn't even want to be an actor and she'd be a much better Wendy than me."

Cosmo said nothing. But he had been secretly shocked by what he'd found at the Swan. He was used to people praising him and telling him how he had inherited the Wood family talent and what a star he was, but he had soon realised that at the Swan he was nothing special. He probably wouldn't even get in if he tried. It made him feel really insecure.

"Look," said Alicia soothingly. "I can't cram five years of training into a few weeks.

But in the time we've got I can teach you some techniques to help you when you get out there in front of an audience."

"I can't do it," said Cosi matter-of-factly. "I can't go out there. I'll just freeze. I'd rather die."

"Oh, Cosi, of course you can do this," said Alicia. "I would never have taken you both on if I didn't think that you could, and you'll be surrounded on stage by people who want you to succeed, not to fail. The audience will be on your side too. They'll want to have a good time, they'll feel sympathetic towards you. But you're going to have to work very hard if we're going to pull this off. Are you willing to do that?"

Cosmo nodded; Cosima looked doubtful but shrugged and said, "I haven't got much choice, have I?" Then she added, "Look, sorry, I know you're really trying to help us, Miss Swan."

"Right then," said Alicia. "Let's not stop. Let's carry on for a few more minutes."

After she had finished working with the twins, Alicia made her way up to the flat and sat down at the kitchen table with her head in her hands. She was exhausted. She was worried about the twins but she was even more worried about the noise from the building site next door. One of the reasons she had been working with the twins after school was that the level of noise was so intense during the day that almost all the classes were severely disrupted. Cosmo had even complained to his dad, and Jasper Wood had given Alicia a hard time. But there didn't seem to be anything that she could do about it, even though the noise was sometimes so intense it felt like a physical assault. Alicia had developed an almost constant headache. She and Sebastian had tried to enter the derelict building but all the entrances seemed to be boarded up. They had never seen anyone go in or out either.

In desperation, Alicia had rung the local planning department to complain about the noise, and had been put through to Bill Jukes, the head of planning, who'd been most unhelpful. He said that nobody else had complained and what did she expect from a building site? He pointed out that she'd had plenty of time to object before the building work started and that it was too late now.

Alicia had been furious. "But I didn't know that work *was* going to start!" she'd said. "I still don't even know what's being built over there."

"Well, you were sent a letter, Miss Swan, and notices went up on all the lamp-posts."

"Well, I never got a letter and I haven't seen any notices," said Alicia.

"That's impossible," said Bill Jukes smoothly. "I arranged it all myself." And before Alicia could say another word, he'd put the phone down. It was all so frustrating.

Up in one of the rehearsal rooms, Olivia, Eel, Tom, Georgia and Aeysha were sitting on the floor eating liquorice laces even though no food was really allowed.

"I've never seen Gran like this before," said Olivia. "It's as if she's completely defeated. I've always thought of her as being like a piece of steel. Unbreakable. I'm really worried."

"We all are," said Tom. "She totally lost it with Will Todd today when he produced that mouse from his pocket in the middle of classical acting class, and normally he always makes her smile however cheeky he is."

"Poor Miss Swan, the pressure is really getting to her," said Georgia. "If only we could help in some way."

"Maybe we could get Jasper Wood to adopt you and Tom, Georgia, and then you could play Peter and Wendy instead of the twins?" said Eel.

"I wish people would be kinder about the twins. It's not their fault they're playing Peter and Wendy; they weren't given any choice by their dad." Olivia had told the others about her awful evening at the Savoy. "Anyway, it's not just the twins who are giving Gran grief, the noise is getting to her too."

"It's getting to all of us," said Tom.

"It really is," said Eel. "Pablo is teaching the trapeze wearing earmuffs and a terrible frown, and my dancing has gone right downhill. My feet can't think when my ears can't hear the music."

"Must you always just think of yourself?" snapped Olivia. Then she looked stricken. "I'm sorry, Eel, I'm a snappy crocodile today. I think it's the noise too. At least it's stopped now."

"Yes, it has, hasn't it?" said Tom. "Don't you think it's funny that it always stops as soon as school ends?"

"I suppose the workmen go home at the same time as school finishes," said Georgia.

Tom looked thoughtful. "But why would

they keep school hours? And why do we never see anyone coming in and out? When they were building that office block down the road, we used to see the workmen everywhere, sitting on the side of the road eating their sandwiches in their bright-yellow hats, buying tea from the café across the road. But this lot are like phantoms."

"That building's been derelict for ages. Maybe it's haunted?" said Eel.

"More likely there just aren't many workmen in there," said Aeysha.

"Well, they make enough noise," said Georgia. "It sounds as if there are hundreds of them."

"It does," said Tom. "What's more, their working hours seem entirely synchronised with the Swan's school day. When we start, the noise starts. When we stop for break or lunch, the noise stops and then as soon as the bell goes again, the noise starts up. I wish we could take a look at what's going on over there."

Olivia looked thoughtful. She opened her mouth to say something, then noticed the time. "Oh!" she cried. "I've got to go!"

"Where?" asked Georgia.

"Oh, I just arranged to meet someone," she said. "I'll tell you about it later." And with that, Olivia dashed out of the room.

Chapter Nine

Olivia took another sip of her orange juice and watched the pigeons in the Covent Garden piazza. Katie Wilkes-Cox was sitting opposite her, talking in a low, urgent voice. It was only a few weeks since Olivia had last seen Katie but she had changed so much. She looked nervous and kept peering about her as if she was worried they were being watched. She had lost the glossy look that had always made her resemble a sleek, pampered cat when she had been at the Swan.

"So we've got to get inside that building and find out exactly what he's up to," concluded Katie. In normal circumstances, Olivia would have dismissed what Katie had been saying as some kind of fabrication but it chimed with Tom's suspicions about a sinister reason for the noise coming from the building next door. Katie was suggesting it wasn't just normal building-site noise but deliberate harassment.

"But why would your dad be doing this, Katie?" asked Olivia.

"That's easy. For starters: revenge. He still has a grudge against Miss Swan for kicking me out. But the other is money. If there's one thing that motivates my dad, it's dosh. Buying this building killed two birds with one stone. He knew that Miss Swan wanted it to expand the school and he liked being able to thwart her. Particularly as he'd previously tried to bribe her to keep me on at the Swan by suggesting he buy it and develop the top half into luxury flats and allow the Swan to expand into the bottom half."

"How generous of him," said Olivia.

"Oh, there'd have been a profit in it for him," said Katie. "There always is. Anyway, he managed to buy the building but then he discovered that there's a new high-speed train link being planned, which will link up to the nearest station. The price of land round here is going to rocket. So he wants the Swan site too. He's made an offer through some business associates." She wrinkled her pretty button nose.

"Not nice people. But your gran doesn't want to sell, and my dad doesn't take no for an answer. So he's going to drive her out if necessary. And he will, Livy. I know him. He'll stop at nothing. He's ruthless when it comes to money."

"Poor Gran," whispered Olivia. No wonder Alicia was so stressed. "Why are you telling me all this, Katie?" she asked quietly.

"I want to help," said Katie. "He boasts about it quite openly at home. Even my mum is sickened, but she's afraid of him. I knew I had to do something. I couldn't just stand by and watch while he tried to destroy the Swan. I had to act. Even if he is my dad, what he's doing is so wrong. He's got to be stopped."

"How do I know I can trust you?" asked Olivia. She knew from bitter experience that Katie was a superb actress who was adept at double dealing and appearing sincere when she was at her most devious. Even Alicia had almost been taken in by Katie's wide-eyed innocent act.

"I don't blame you for being suspicious, Livy," said Katie sadly. "I know I haven't earned your trust, but I will be forever grateful to you for what you and Tom did. You saved my life. Nothing will ever be enough, but the least I can do is try to save the Swan. I didn't realise it at the time, but it's the only place I've ever been happy. I squandered all that but I can't sit back and let my dad destroy the school. But that means getting into the building and he's certainly not going to give me the key. Then I thought of you. You can get in."

Olivia looked into Katie's face. She wanted so much to believe that Katie was telling her the truth but a tiny part of her brain kept telling her, *You know what she's like. Don't trust her. Don't allow yourself to be taken in.* She pushed the thought away.

"We've got to get into the building," said Katie insistently, "and you're the only person I know who can do it, Livy."

Olivia swallowed. In her first term she had risked her life by walking a wire stretched across the gap from the Swan to the derelict building next door to retrieve some jewellery from the nest of a bird that had stolen it. If she had fallen off, she'd have plunged to her death. Afterwards, she had promised her gran that she'd never do anything so dangerous again. But she had added a proviso: "Unless I feel I really have to." Well, she did have to. She couldn't bear to see

Gran lose everything she'd worked so hard for. She had to find out what was happening in that building.

"Could you go in over the roof?" asked Katie. Olivia nodded. "Then you can let me in. It's only a Chubb lock. I've seen the key."

"That's decided then," said Olivia. "We'll do it." She couldn't tell whether the feeling inside her tummy was excitement or fear. Fear that Katie could not be trusted.

The entire class was in the computer suite. They were supposed to be researching their projects on famous scientists. Olivia and Cosi had been assigned Sir Isaac Newton. Cosi had never heard of him and all Olivia could remember was that he had had something to do with apples. Tom and Cosmo were given Galileo. Cosmo insisted this was the name of a new American boy band and was showing Tom their website.

Olivia was distracted. She was thinking about her conversation with Katie. Was she being led into some kind of trap? Either way, she knew she had to do something. She'd told Jack about the noise but because he was never around during school hours he really had no idea how bad it was and had thought that she was exaggerating. She wondered about going to the police herself, but what would she say? She had a strange feeling that Alicia would deny she was being threatened. It was clear that her gran was very frightened indeed.

Olivia dragged her attention back to the computer. Cosi was hunched over the screen muttering furiously to herself, but when Olivia looked over her shoulder she saw she was on the World Wildlife Fund site. That didn't seem to have anything to do with Newton or apples. Cosi clicked on a picture of a polar bear with her cubs.

"Er, Cosi," said Olivia. "I don't think Sir Isaac Newton had white fur and a big black nose. Cute pic though."

"Oh, Livy, it's so sad!" Cosi turned to her and for the first time Olivia saw something like passion burning in her eyes. "In about a hundred years, if we don't do something about global warming, there'll be no polar bears left because the ice is melting and they'll have nowhere to live!" Cosi looked almost as fierce as a polar bear herself.

"That's terrible!" said Olivia.

"And it's not just polar bears – it's seals as well, and all sorts of other species. Maybe even us too! I've been reading about it. By the end of the century, Bangladesh will be under water and the Maldives will have disappeared. Whole countries, just disappearing." Olivia wasn't entirely sure where the Maldives were but she couldn't imagine what it would be like to lose her home. It made her feel terrible.

"How come you know about this and I don't?" asked Olivia, although she had a vague memory of Jack and Alicia sitting talking one night over Christmas about rising sea levels and temperatures.

"I look on websites, and I've got some books too," said Cosi. "It's all really scary. It makes me want to do something. Look at this!" She clicked on a link and Olivia quickly scanned the screen.

"See?" said Cosi. "Earth is our home but we're destroying it. We're trashing the planet. There must be something we can do but I don't know what."

Olivia suddenly had a brilliant idea. "But, Cosi, you're famous! Everyone would listen to you. Instead of using the Wood name to sell stuff, you could use it to tell people about the polar bears and what we're doing to our home."

"As if. Dad would never let me do anything like that," said Cosi miserably. "He says the Woods are about acting and nothing else. Besides, you've seen the way we live. My family never walk anywhere. Not if we can go by limo or private jet. I wanted to use some of my money to plant trees to offset the carbon emissions of all the flying we do but Dad said no way. He said it's not his problem, but it is – it's everyone's problem."

"Oh, come on, Cosi! You're just allowing yourself to be defeated," said Olivia quite sharply. "My dad always says there's no point talking the talk unless you can walk the walk too." For a moment, Cosi looked as if Olivia had slapped her, but then she suddenly jumped up and threw her arms out wide. She appeared to be about to address a big crowd. "It's all our problem, and I can do something, and you're right, I *must* and I *will* do something. I can help save the polar bears!"

Everyone in the class looked up. Cosi's eyes were blazing with passion. She was a very different Cosi from the one who looked nervous and mumbled all the time.

Cosmo rolled his eyes. "Quit going on about the stupid polar bears, will you? Who cares? All that stuff's just for hippies."

"I care," said Olivia.

"Me too," said Georgia, and loads of other people joined in as well. Cosi started telling the class about melting polar ice caps and rising sea levels. Mrs Wren, the teacher, didn't stop her. After all, Cosi was talking about science and lots of people in the class were clearly interested. And she was remarkably well informed. Cosi drew breath and moved on to trees and how important they were to the earth's ecology.

As she listened, Olivia found herself admiring the intensity of Cosi's feelings. She had never really felt passionate about an issue that didn't directly affect her, although she had a lot of respect for Aeysha, who had become a vegetarian because she didn't think you should eat anything that you weren't prepared to kill yourself. Eel had asked if sausages counted as you didn't have to hunt them down and kill them, and although everyone had laughed, they all admired Aeysha for taking a stand. Now Cosi was trying to do the same. It was hard to worry about stuff that might not happen for years, by which time she might even be dead. But Cosi's passion was infectious, and Olivia suddenly felt quite fired up too.

The bell rang and Cosi stopped speaking. "Thank you," Mrs Wren told her. "You've taught us all a great deal. If anyone wants to find out more I've got some books you can borrow." Several people put their hands up.

"See, Cosi," said Olivia. "You've made a difference already."

Chapter Ten

Olivia and Tom soared out over the empty auditorium of the Imperial theatre one last time. Olivia stretched out her arms as if she was a bird. It was exhilarating. They swung back towards the stage and were gently lowered down by the stage crew using a series of weights and counterweights that made it look as if they were swooping seamlessly to the ground just like real birds.

"Thanks!" they chorused to the stagehands as they helped them unclip their safety harnesses.

"What a smooth landing!" said Tom. "That was such fun. It's a great way to spend Saturday morning. Better than doing maths homework. It's a pity Georgia and Aeysha couldn't come."

Jon James gave Jack a thumbs-up and

clapped him on the back. "It's brilliant, Jack. I've never seen such realistic flying in the theatre. Your system really does work. I'm sorry I doubted you after seeing the twins fly. The problem's obviously with them, not the equipment."

"Don't worry," replied Jack. "It's not so very different from what theatres have been using for over a hundred years. I just made a few tweaks, and don't forget that Liv and Tom are real naturals in the air and completely fearless. Sometimes worryingly fearless, particularly Liv. Cosmo and Cosi just need to build their confidence, then they'll look less like sacks of potatoes and more as if they've been sprinkled with fairy dust."

"Hmm," said Jon grimly. "It's a pity that none of their people thought to mention that Cosi is afraid of heights. You would have thought they'd realise that playing Wendy would involve flying."

"It's not the poor kid's fault," said Jack. "She's not had a normal childhood. I don't think she's ever been allowed to do anything other than work. You know where the Swan's grounds meet the river? Well, Liv and Eel and their friends took the twins tree-climbing there yesterday, and apparently they just looked at the trees completely baffled and said, 'We don't know how to. Nobody's ever taught us.' You'd laugh if it wasn't so tragic. What child needs to be taught to climb a tree? It's something you find out how to do by doing it."

"I haven't climbed a tree for years," said Jon wistfully. "I don't know why I stopped."

"You grew up, Jon," replied Jack. "One of the things I love about having kids is I can carry on doing all the things I enjoyed as a child."

"OK, let's try and get the twins up there again now they've seen how it can be done," said Jon. He called out to the stagehands, "Ready crew for flying sequence. Cosmo and Cosima on stage, please. Livy and Tom, can you help them?"

"Cosi?" said Olivia.

Cosi reluctantly put down her magazine and came over. "It makes me sick," she said.

"You'll stop feeling queasy when you've been up a few times," said Olivia soothingly.

"I don't mean the flying," she replied. "I've been doing some more research. Mrs Wren showed me some more websites and gave me this magazine. At the end of last summer there was a third less sea ice in the North Pole as there was in 1979. If you're a polar bear, it means you have to swim further to find food and you get a whole lot more tired. Some even drown. It also means that they don't have as much body fat and the females can't feed their cubs properly so they grow up weaker than they should. And the worst thing is nobody cares."

"You do, Cosi," said Olivia as one of the stagehands fastened Cosi's safety harness.

"Yes, but I'm still not doing anything about it even after everything I said in class. I'm like everyone else; I do nothing even though I know more so I've less excuse," said Cosi sadly.

"You'll find a way," said Olivia before she was interrupted by a loud shout.

"You're strangling me, you jackass!" said Cosmo angrily. Cosmo's minder rushed over and glowered at the stagehand. The stagehand, a nice man called Gary with years of experience, backed away.

"You know, I think you need to have a word with your brother, Cosi," said Tom seriously. "He treats the stagehands as if they're servants, but they're not. They're professionals and his life is in their hands. He wouldn't want them to drop him mid-air, would he?"

"Oh my gosh, they wouldn't, would they?" asked Cosi, looking terrified.

"No, of course not," laughed Tom. "But they can give you a hard time up there. There was a famous actress who had a big bust up with the stagehands while she was playing Peter Pan. But they had their revenge at the next performance. Instead of lowering her gently into the Darling nursery they bounced her off the walls like a wrecking ball on a building site."

"I bet she was really nice to them after that," said Olivia.

"She was," said Tom. "She had to have a few performances off. But when she came back she treated them like royalty."

"I think we'd better warn Cosmo immediately," said Cosi.

"Everybody ready?" called Jon. The stagehands nodded. "OK, let's fly!"

Cosmo and Cosima were hauled upwards. Cosi screamed and even Cosmo looked uncertain. They were pushed out over the auditorium flapping their arms like a couple of frightened ducks. Cosmo made a sudden movement, lost all control and started bouncing up and down like a baby in a baby bouncer, before going into a spin and squawking loudly. The twins' minders were getting agitated. Olivia and Tom looked at each other and tried not to laugh.

"I'm going to throw up," warned Cosi.

"Oh no you're not," boomed Jasper Wood, who was striding down the centre aisle with Alicia following behind him. Jasper looked rather dashing, wearing a full-length leather coat. "Remember who you are. You are Wendy and you are flying to Never Land on an awfully big adventure. Quit complaining and start acting. It's what we Woods do."

Cosi opened her mouth to reply, made a strangulated noise and was promptly sick all over her father, who was standing right below. Jasper looked murderous and if he'd had a cutlass would probably have shaken it at his daughter. Olivia and Tom were convulsed with giggles.

"Ah!" muttered Jack. "I think that all flights are probably grounded for the rest of the day."

Half an hour later Jon, Jack and Alicia were

sitting alone together in the Green Room. Jon had his head in his hands. "They can't act. They can't fly. What *can* they do?"

"They look absolutely lovely," said Alicia soothingly. "Don't blame the twins, Jon. They're being asked to give more than they can possibly deliver. Cosi is already well aware of her limitations and Cosmo is far too self-confident, although he does show sparks of real potential. You're just going to have to be really ingenious, and think of the box office. I've heard that *Peter Pan* is the fastest-selling show in West End history."

"We'll have to give it all back if we have to cancel the show. The investors will lose every penny and none of us will ever work in the West End again," groaned Jon. "Thank goodness for the Swans. At least I've seen some real talent at the auditions for the other children's roles."

"I have a proposal," said Jack. "Two, actually. First of all, I'm going to show all the children who have to fly exactly how the system works. If I show Cosi all the mechanics behind it and which ropes and wires are responsible for which actions, maybe it will make her less nervous. She won't think she's being held up by

100

magic and can relax a bit."

"That could help," said Jon. "What's your other proposal?"

"We ask Liv really nicely and, if she says yes, we bring her in as a flying double for Cosi. Only for the more difficult sequences such as soaring out over the auditorium and when Wendy gets shot down by the Lost Boys because Tinkerbell tells them that's what Peter wants. At least let's use her for the previews and the first few weeks until Cosi's really got her confidence. Nobody need ever know. Liv and Cosi are similar builds and they're nearly the same height. It will be one less thing for you and Cosi to worry about."

Jon had visibly brightened, but then a frown crossed his face again. "That's all great, Jack, but it doesn't solve the problem of Cosmo. That was like watching an elephant trying to fly."

"Well," said Alicia, "I think I might have an answer for you there too. Why not get Tom to hold his hand? Literally and metaphorically. Release him from the last few performances of *The Sound of Music* and cast him as John in *Peter Pan*. I know you've seen lots of children, but you haven't cast the role yet. He'd be brilliant and you'd have somebody you really trust to help Cosmo with the flying and the acting. You need to surround the twins with people who you know will deliver and who will help them with their confidence."

"Alicia, you are a genius! Let's do it," said Jon excitedly.

"You'll have to ask Livy and Tom yourself, Jon; I can't speak for them," said Alicia. "They may not want to do it."

"Livy won't mind not getting to act?" asked Jon.

"Goodness no," said Alicia. "I don't think she'll care. She *is* an actress but she just doesn't know it yet. She has to find out for herself, and she hasn't as yet, although it's only a matter of time. She'll just love working alongside her dad."

"I don't suppose I could have Eel as well?" asked Jon wistfully. "She'd make a brilliantly stroppy Tinkerbell. It would be great publicity. A complete set of Woods and a complete set of Marvells."

"She would indeed be a delicious Tinkerbell, but I think you might be pushing your luck," replied Alicia. "Eel is currently dedicating her life to dancing with commendable zeal and doesn't need or want any distractions. Besides," she added with a twinkle, "I don't think Eel believes in fairies. The only thing Eel really believes in is Eel."

Chapter Eleven

Olivia leaned out over the window sill of the Swan's upper rehearsal room and threw the end of the wire over the spike sticking out of the roof of the derelict building next door. It caught first time. She had become adept at lassoing the spike during her first term when she had used the upper rehearsal room as a place to practise the high-wire in secret, convinced that everyone at the Swan hated the circus.

It was Monday evening and it was starting to get dark. Tom, who had agreed to join the *Peter Pan* cast with Olivia, was in his final week of *The Sound of Music*, but he and Georgia had Monday nights off because they played the Sunday matinée. Georgia only had two more weeks and then she'd be free every evening too. Jack was working late at the theatre; he'd come up with a novel idea for how they could represent Tinkerbell on stage and he and Jon wanted to try it out. Eel had gone to have supper with her friend Emmy, and Olivia had told Alicia, who had gone to *Billy Elliot* to check up on some of the Swan children, that she and her friends were working on a scene for Sebastian Shaw's acting class. She felt a twinge of guilt for telling Alicia a lie.

Olivia's phone bleeped. It was a message from Katie saying that she was outside the derelict building waiting for Olivia to let her in. Olivia texted back to say she was on her way. It was time to walk the wire.

"Liv, are you really sure this is a good idea?" asked Tom. "When you did it last time you had a really good reason, and when we risked our lives walking between the New Vic Theatre and the Duke's it was an emergency situation. It doesn't feel that there's so much at stake now."

"It does to me," said Olivia fiercely. "You didn't see Gran this afternoon. She had tears in her eyes. And I heard her talking to Sebastian Shaw. A lot of parents have been complaining about the noise. Some have even been threatening to withhold this term's fees. She said that she was thinking of temporarily closing the school down and renting somewhere just for morning academic lessons. That's not like Gran at all. For Gran, the show always goes on, whatever happens."

Georgia saw the determination in Olivia's face. She turned to the others. "We won't persuade Olivia not to do it so I think the best thing is to give her whatever support we can," she said.

"Just you being here is what I need," said Olivia.

"I'm going to come with you, Liv. I can't let you go alone," said Tom.

Olivia looked at his open, freckled face and thought how lucky she was to have a friend so loyal and supportive. She shook her head. "No, Tom, you're not. Only one of us needs to take the risk. It's my idea and I'm the one going across. You can help me best by staying here and keeping a watch out for Gran in case she comes back unexpectedly. Oh, and if I don't come back after a while you can go and get help."

Olivia clambered up on to the window sill.

She turned round and added, "Besides, I'm not going to be alone in the building. I'm going to let someone else in."

"Who?" demanded Georgia.

"Katie Wilkes-Cox." If Olivia had just lobbed a small bomb into the room it could not have had a more explosive effect. Her friends all looked appalled.

"You can't be serious, Liv?" said Tom.

"I am though. Perfectly serious," said Olivia. "Her dad has bought the building. She thinks he's trying to close the Swan down, and that's why we're going to get inside and find out exactly what he's up to. Then we can stop it."

"How do you know all this?" asked Aeysha.

"She texted me a couple of times and then I went to meet her," said Olivia.

"But how can you be sure it's not some kind of elaborate trick? A Katie Wilkes-Cox special?" asked Tom.

"I can't be sure," said Olivia. "I just have to trust my instincts and believe that she really has changed."

"And if it's a trap?" asked Georgia.

"I'll be relying on you three to bail me out

in whatever way you can. Pass me that torch," she said. She took it from Ayesha, slung it round her neck and stepped out on to the wire.

"Good luck!" called Aeysha.

"Take care, Liv," said Tom.

"Don't look down," said Georgia helpfully. Tom and Aeysha frowned at her. "Sorry, Livy. It just popped out because I'm nervous."

But Olivia was grinning, even although they couldn't see her face. "I'll try and follow your advice, Georgia," she called into the wind. She felt so sure that everything was going to be all right.

As soon as she stepped on to it, the wire sagged slightly. Olivia shifted her balance and then walked quickly along the wire. Georgia and Aeysha both held their breath. It never failed to amaze them the way that Olivia walked the wire as if she had completely solid ground beneath her feet. It didn't seem to matter to her that she was over thirty metres up in the air; she behaved as if she was taking a stroll in the park.

Her friends all breathed again when Olivia reached the surround of the building opposite and tensed as she negotiated her way over the parapet and on to the roof. Olivia scrambled upwards towards a small battered-looking window and perched on the raked roof. She took a screwdriver out of her pocket and slid it into the frame of the window. It gave easily. She had to duck slightly to avoid the edge of the window as she pulled it outwards and then she scrambled over the sill. Once inside she switched on her torch, blew the others a kiss and then disappeared.

Inside the building, Olivia shivered as she looked around her. It was a warmish spring evening but the building felt cold and damp as years of neglect had taken their toll. It was very dark inside and she was glad of the torch, but it was still a gloomy and scary place to be on your own. The top floor of the building must once have been used by a business as it was divided into offices. In some of the rooms there were still desks and chairs, and great old metal filing cabinets, their drawers hanging open and empty. On some desks there were a few discarded files covered in dust, some splattered with pigeon droppings. There were even a few old mugs left on desks as if their owners had just been called away, and one desk boasted an empty crisp packet and a desiccated plant.

Above it was pinned an old calendar, a faded good-luck card and a photo of a long-forgotten office Christmas party in which everyone was wearing silly hats.

It reminded Olivia of the time that she and Eel and Jack had been in Italy and they'd visited Pompeii. The city had been destroyed by the volcanic eruption of Mount Vesuvius in AD 79 and had been preserved under layers of ash. She had experienced the eerie feeling that the dead from all those centuries ago might return at any moment to reclaim their houses and carry on with what they had been doing the moment before catastrophe struck and they were suddenly engulfed by lava. She got the same feeling now and even wondered if the building might be haunted.

Olivia took a few steps and the floor creaked badly. She knew that she had to be careful because the floor could have rotted in places. Take a wrong step and she might plunge through to the floor below. She took a good look around and felt rather puzzled. There was no sign of any building work going on here. If you were going to start work on a building like this, either to restore it or demolish it, surely the first thing you'd do was empty it out completely? She headed towards the stairs that led down to the next floor and as she did so, something flashed past her. She gave a little cry of fear and her heart began to boom, feeling as if it had suddenly become too big for her chest. She swung her torch wildly around and found a startled pigeon sitting entirely unperturbed on one of the rafters, watching her. She was so relieved that she sank down on to the top step for a moment. She wished she'd accepted Tom's offer to come with her. They'd both be laughing together now, while instead she was feeling mighty nervous. Walking the wire had been the easy part. The building felt as if it was about to spring a nasty surprise on her. She stood up carefully and started down the stairs.

It was darker on the floor below but she could see immediately that the partitions had been cleared and it was almost empty. Where, she wondered, was all the heavy machinery that was causing such disruption to the Swan? But she could see some things stacked in the middle of the room, so she shone the beam of her torch over them. There was a lot of recording equipment, with lights winking on and off all over it, and some massive speakers, bigger than she'd ever seen in her life. There were also what looked like alarm clocks all over the place. It was very odd. She wondered if someone was planning some kind of illegal warehouse party and hoped it wasn't going to be tonight. The last thing Gran needed was to be kept awake all night.

She listened hard. She was certain she was quite alone in the building. Then her phone bleeped and she guessed it was an impatient Katie wanting to know where she was. She stepped forwards and something small and furry ran over her foot. Olivia screamed and her hand came down hard on a button that said "Play". Suddenly the room was filled with a roar of machinery so unbearably loud that Olivia was almost knocked backwards. Her ears hadn't experienced such pain since she was three and had had a terrible ear infection that needed antibiotics. She fumbled for the stop button and pressed it. For the second time in just a few minutes she sank to the floor. She stayed there quietly for several minutes while her brain worked overtime. She knew now that there was to be no warehouse party; this was all part of Mr

Wilkes-Cox's plan.

Olivia headed carefully down to the next floor. Its layout was the same as the one above and she wasn't at all surprised to find the same arrangement of outsized speakers facing towards the Swan and the same recording equipment and timers. She ignored them and hurried down the stairs to the ground floor. She opened the door and for a moment felt afraid but all she found was a nervous-looking Katie Wilkes-Cox.

"Quick, shut the door!" said Katie as she slipped in. "What took you so long and what was that terrible noise?"

"Come and see what I've found," said Olivia, leading the way up the stairs. Katie turned her torch on and followed Olivia to the first floor.

"Look," said Olivia, shining her torch over the equipment. The beam settled on the timers, and immediately she realised that they were set to coincide with the starts and stops of the Swan school day. Mr Wilkes-Cox was using noise as a weapon.

"Wow," said Katie. "You do have to hand it to my dad – he may entirely lack a conscience or a heart but he is very, very smart." She sounded despairing. "We've got to find a way to stop him."

"Ssh!" whispered Olivia urgently. "What was that noise?"

Chapter Twelve

Over in the Swan, Tom, Aeysha and Georgia jumped at the sudden burst of machinery noise. They stared at each other fearfully. The roar ceased almost as soon as it had begun.

"Somebody must be in there with Liv and Katie!" said Tom. "I'm going to go over to find out what's going on."

"No, Tom," said Georgia. "It's too dangerous. Whoever is in there has obviously already found them poking around. Maybe there was some kind of night watchman we didn't know about."

"Or maybe Katie betrayed Olivia; maybe it was all a set-up? After all, Katie's got form in that department," said Aeysha quietly.

Georgia gasped.

"Whatever it is, Livy's going to get into terrible trouble and you don't want to get caught too, Tom. She won't thank you if you give away the fact she went into the building on the wire," said Aeysha.

"Do you think they'll call the police and have Livy arrested?" asked Georgia tearfully.

"It'll be Miss Swan who'll have Livy under lock and key, particularly if she discovers how she got into the building. She'll be furious," said Aeysha.

Georgia tried to sound hopeful. "Maybe they'll just let her go? Why don't we go downstairs and wait for her just in case? At least we'll be there to see if the police do turn up to arrest her," said Georgia. Ayesha nodded.

"I'm going to stay here," said Tom. "In case she comes back this way."

The others left. He got out his mobile and stared at it. He knew that Liv had her phone with her. He wondered whether he should try calling her. He was desperate to find out what was happening but what if they were wrong and Katie hadn't betrayed her and she hadn't been discovered? He didn't want to do anything that might put her in danger.

* * *

Olivia and Katie stared at each other in the gloom. They had both gone so pale that they looked like ghosts. There was somebody else in the building. They could hear whoever it was moving about downstairs.

"It was a trap," said Olivia in a dazed whisper. "I believed you, Katie. I trusted you and you betrayed me. You're just the same Katie you've always been."

"No, Livy!" whispered back Katie. "I promise. It's not like that. I *have* changed. I'd never do anything to hurt you. Please believe me. It'll be my dad, come to check the equipment. I didn't know he was coming, honest. I thought he was safely tied up in a meeting tonight."

She turned off her torch and pulled Olivia towards two huge filing cabinets standing side by side by the wall. Olivia switched her torch off too. She was shivering with fear. She didn't know whether to believe Katie or not.

They crouched behind the filing cabinets in the dark, hardly daring to breathe. They heard footsteps coming up the stairs, then Mr Wilkes-Cox walked into the room. He swung his torch around the room and then went over to his equipment.

"Looks good," he muttered to himself. "Another nice peaceful day ahead for the Swan." He turned to walk up the stairs to the next floor when Olivia's mobile went off. Katie's dad swung round and shouted, "Who's there?"

Olivia felt Katie squeeze her hand as she stepped out from behind the filing cabinet and said, "It's all right, Dad, it's only me. My mobile just rang."

Her father was shining the torch right in her eyes.

"Kitten! What on earth are you doing here?" He looked around suspiciously. "Are you on your own?"

"Quite alone, Dad."

"How did you get in?"

"Oh," said Katie, gazing up at him adoringly and putting her arm through his. "I came over this way to see my old friend Kylie Morris. You remember her; we took her on safari with us."

Mr Wilkes-Cox was frowning. "I didn't think you kept in touch with anyone from the Swan."

"Oh, I haven't seen Kylie for ages. She's leaving too. She says lots of people are going. The Swan's losing its reputation." She looked at her dad wide-eyed. "I don't know what you're up to, Dad, but it's definitely working. You are clever."

Momentarily Mr Wilkes-Cox looked pleased, but then wariness clouded his face. "But why on earth would you want to come in here, and how did you get inside a locked building?"

"Well, that's the thing," said Katie. "I was just saying goodbye to Kylie when I noticed that the front door was swinging open. I thought maybe you had accidentally forgotten to lock it. I was going to call you but I thought I'd better check everything was OK. Of course, I did think that maybe I ought to just ring the police, but I wasn't sure if that would be the right thing to do."

Katie sounded as innocent as the first snowdrop of spring. Olivia held her breath. Would Mr Wilkes-Cox fall for it? Katie was acting superbly and sounded remarkably convincing. The bit about the police was a brainwave. The last thing Mr Wilkes-Cox would want was the police asking awkward questions about his equipment.

"Hmm, yes, you were quite right not to call them, Katie," he blustered. "I always think it's best to leave them out of things. They just go poking their noses around where they're not wanted. You should have called me, instead of running around derelict buildings on your own. It's not safe." He put his arm round his daughter and started to steer her towards the stairs. "Well, everything looks as if it's in working order here. The Swan is going to get exactly what it deserves again tomorrow. You go and wait outside, and I'll just have a quick look around to check that nobody else got in while the door was open."

"Oh, they didn't, Dad. I've looked. The building's completely empty apart from a few pigeons. I think you just didn't close the door properly last time you were here and then after a while it blew open. It's quite windy today. It was lucky I was passing."

"Yes, it was, kitten," said Mr Wilkes-Cox. "I'm going to have to bring in some proper security for this place. Let's go home."

"Yes, let's," said Katie, "and you can tell me everything about your plans for the site. I want to know everything you're up to. I hate the stupid Swan. I'd like to see it torn down brick by brick."

Olivia breathed a sigh of relief. She waited until she heard the door of the building bang shut, then stood for a moment uncertain of what to do. If she just left, she would have achieved nothing and as soon as the school day started tomorrow, the Swan would be bombarded with noise. She couldn't bear the thought of her gran's pale, strained face. It made her feel so angry she wanted to smash all the equipment to smithereens. But even if she'd had a hammer, she knew that she wouldn't have used it. It wasn't in her nature to destroy with such cold-minded intent. She stood immobile for a second longer and then she started unplugging all the equipment as fast as she could. Of course Mr Wilkes-Cox could just plug it all in again, but he'd have to come back first and at least he'd know that someone was on to him. It might even win the Swan a few days' respite from the noise. When she had finished, she headed back up the stairs towards the roof, the wire and home.

Georgia and Aeysha raced up the stairs towards the top rehearsal room. Their eyes were wide with panic and their cheeks were flushed from running.

"We saw someone come out of the building," shouted Georgia. "But it wasn't Olivia. You've got to go over there, Tom, and see what's happened to her!"

"It must be something terrible," said Aeysha. "We're so worried."

"Calm down and tell me slowly," said Tom. "Who did you see coming out of the building?"

"Katie Wilkes-Cox. And her dad," said Olivia calmly as she stepped off the wire and ducked under the window frame on to the sill.

"Livy!" cried her friends. "Are you all right?"

"Fine," said Olivia. "I've got a lot to tell you." She explained what she had found in the building.

"Well, at least the Swan will get a bit of peace and quiet," said Olivia. "It really does seem as if Katie genuinely wants to help us. She saved me from her dad. She didn't give me away."

"Maybe a leopard *can* change its spots," said Aeysha.

Chapter Thirteen

"So," said Jack. "I've shown you all the rigging for the flying, and once we've got your parents' permission, every child involved in the production will get a chance to fly if they want to."

A big cheer went up from the assembled children. Olivia, Tom, Cosi and Cosmo, and the boy playing Michael were the envy of the whole cast, who all wanted a go at flying. Jack had organised the workshop on the flying rig for everyone involved in the production but his ulterior motive had been to put the twins at their ease. He'd even managed to persuade Jasper that the twins' minders should stay away from the theatre during the workshop.

"Now you know how safe it is, does anyone

123

have any more questions?"

Cosi put up her hand. Jack was pleased. To his surprise, Cosi had taken a really intelligent interest in the flying rig and had already asked lots of questions. He had been very patient, showing her which wires and ropes were directly connected to her harness and emphasising the care that was taken to check that everything was in order before and during each flight.

"I just wanted to say thanks to Mr Marvell for showing us the ropes," she said.

"You're welcome, Cosi," said Jack. "I just hope you realise now that nobody needs to have a fear of flying. Really. Nothing can go wrong."

Jon was so thrilled to have Tom and Olivia involved in *Peter Pan*, and was feeling so well disposed towards Alicia, Jack and the Swan (which had provided most of the children in the production) that he was doing anything he could to keep them all happy. He hoped that Cosmo and Cosima might relax and perform better if they were having a good time.

Jon had noticed that they were both less stressed when they were away from Jasper and was now beginning to understand Cosima's remark at the press conference. Jasper Wood may not have an iron hook instead of a hand but he could inflict real damage on his children with his sarcasm. Once, when Cosima had forgotten her lines, Jasper had behaved with a brutal, Hook-like coldness. It wasn't hard to believe that, given half the chance, he really would make his daughter walk the plank into a shark-infested sea.

"You're just not making any effort, Cosi," he'd said. "You don't deserve the family name."

"I don't want the family name!" his daughter had screamed back at him. "I don't even want to be an actor! I hate it!"

Alicia, who had been at the theatre, had taken Cosi away to dry her tears.

"Poor little motherless things," she said to Jack, over a late night glass of wine back at her flat. "They're completely afraid of their dad and his insane idea of family duty. Even Cosmo is a seething mass of insecurities beneath that arrogant exterior. Did you know he takes eight different kinds of vitamin pill? That's not normal behaviour for a twelve-year-old." She sighed. "What they desperately need is a mum to stick up for them."

"Liv and Eel don't have a mum to stick up for them," said Jack quietly, looking at the picture of Toni over the mantelpiece. He seldom mentioned his beloved wife. She had married Jack against Alicia's wishes and mother and daughter had only just been reconciled when Toni had been killed. It was a painful subject for them both.

"No," said Alicia, "but Olivia and Eel don't have Jasper Wood as their dad. They have you, Jack, and you're an amazing father. Not a conventional one, it's true, and not one who's there all the time, but one who really does listen to his children, who tells them when they're making mistakes and who is on their side and there for them when it really matters." Alicia looked Jack straight in the eye, recalling the terrible scene that had taken place in this very room only two terms ago when Jack, who had lost his travelling circus due to a road accident, had turned up destitute and asked Alicia to take his daughters in.

"I once called you an unfit father, Jack. I thought you were selfish, irresponsible and reckless and accused you of abandoning your own children. Like a child who had never grown up. I was wrong. Completely wrong. I now realise that you love Livy and Eel very much and that they love you. The three of you have an incredible bond. You've done a really good job of raising those girls on your own. Toni would be proud of you, Jack, and so I am. Very proud." Alicia had tears in her eyes, and Jack knew that it had cost her a great deal to say what she had said.

"That's one of the nicest things anyone has ever said to me, Alicia. Thank you," he said quietly.

There was a pause before the conversation moved on.

"Pablo told me the noise from the building site next door has stopped," said Jack. "That must be a big relief."

"Yes, it is," replied Alicia, though she still looked anxious. "But I don't suppose it will last."

Jack looked at her troubled face. "Alicia, is there something else worrying you?" he asked. Alicia swallowed and using all her acting skills she shook her head very firmly.

The next day Jon had organised a huge picnic

for all the *Peter Pan* children. After seeing how well the twins, particularly Cosi, had responded in the workshop when the minders weren't present, Jon had persuaded Jasper to get rid of them permanently. He was pleased that he had. Jasper would have had a fit if it had been reported back to him how his children were spending their afternoon.

The children spent a couple of hours on the riverbank at the back of the Swan, climbing trees and pretending to be pirates. It was great fun and everybody was getting on brilliantly. Jack, Pablo and a couple of the stagehands fashioned a zip-wire between a couple of the trees, which all the children loved except Cosi and Cosmo, who refused to go on it. Cosi was frightened, but Cosmo thought that his dad wouldn't approve.

Tom caught Cosmo looking wistfully at the others as they slid screaming down the wire. "Come on, Cosmo, why don't you have a go? Your dad'll never know. There's nobody to tell him now that your minders have gone."

Cosmo grinned and headed for the wire. Soon he was zipping up and down and Tom showed him how to climb to the top of one of the tallest trees, too. He was good at it. His head could be seen bobbing about among the leaves alongside Tom's red head and Aeysha's dark one.

"I hope Cosmo doesn't get stuck or we'll have to call the fire brigade to rescue him," said Jon nervously.

"Don't worry," said Jack. "He's having the time of his life. Let him enjoy himself. Tom and Aeysha will look after him. He really does seem to be behaving like a kid, not a mini-adult. I saw him actually eating a sandwich and a cupcake instead of that green gloop he swallows all the time."

"Even Cosi looks happier," said Jon.

"Yes," said Jack. "And she seemed to take a real interest in the flying equipment at the workshop. I hope I've set her mind at rest about how safe it is and she can relax a little."

Olivia rather wished that she was climbing trees with Tom and the others too, but she was trying to be a good friend to Cosima.

"The trees are so beautiful," said Cosi, biting into a cheese and watercress sandwich. "It's amazing to think that some of them have probably been here for hundreds of years."

"So they're even older than Gran," said

Eel, quite wide-eyed.

"Much older, Eel," said Cosi. "And lots of creatures and plants will be living on them. Even fungi."

"Gran definitely doesn't have any fungi growing on her," said Eel.

"No," laughed Cosi, "but because trees support other life, every single one is precious."

"But there are masses of them," said Eel. "Why does it matter if one or two get chopped down?"

"It matters because seventy per cent of the earth's animals and plants live in forests," said Cosi seriously. "Cut down a tree and you cut down their home. How would you like it if somebody came along and pulled your house down just because they wanted to?"

Olivia, who had been listening quietly up till then, said fiercely, "I'd hate it. I'd fight as hard as I could to stop them."

"So would I," said Cosi. "And that's why we have to fight on behalf of the animals and plants who can't fight for themselves. Otherwise the trees will disappear. At the rate things are going, by this time next century there will be no rainforest left at all."

Eel goggled at them. "I can't think that far ahead," she said. "And that's enough gloomy stuff. I want another go on the zip-wire. I'm very good at it. I'm better than lots of the boys." She ran away followed by William Todd, who had been cast as Tootles in *Peter Pan*.

"Selfish little beast; she never thinks of anyone but herself," laughed Olivia affectionately. "She's heartless just like Peter Pan and she boasts about how great she is just like him too."

"Livy," said Cosi shyly, now they were left alone. "Have you ever acted on a big stage in front of a huge audience?"

"I've really not done a lot of acting," said Olivia. "I used to think it was silly and pointless. But I don't think that now. I like it more and more. It's cool. But mostly I do circus stuff. But I did play Juliet in a version of *Romeo and Juliet* on the high-wire at the London Palladium and that was massive and I loved it."

"I bet you were really good at it," said Cosima plaintively. "I've heard you when you're helping Cosmo run through his lines. You're fantastic as Wendy. Cosmo much prefers acting opposite you, I can tell. He's much better as Peter when you're being Wendy in those little bits you do for me. In fact, he's really good. I wish you were playing Wendy and not me. I know all the Swan children in the cast do too. I hear them whispering."

"You worry too much, Cosi. Nobody thinks that, nobody whispers about you and you're going to be fine. Gran's been saying how well you're coming along. And you're already so experienced. You've had your own TV show and you've made movies. When you walk out on stage for the first preview with the audience out front you'll forget all your worries and you'll just be Wendy and you'll be brilliant."

Cosi grimaced. "Or I'll make a complete fool of myself. TV and movies are different. You can retake the scene. It once took me sixty-two takes to get one line right. You can't do that in the theatre, and the audience is out there in the dark, just waiting for you to make a mistake. Just like the crocodile with its jaws open waiting for Captain Hook. I can't do it. I keep hoping the end of the world will arrive before the first preview."

"Oh, Cosi, it will be all right on the night, I'm sure it will. Once you've done it the first time it will be a breeze," said Olivia. "What does your dad think about all this?"

Cosi laughed bitterly. "What do you think? He just doesn't listen and he wouldn't care if he did."

Chapter Fourteen

Eel, Tom and Cosmo were laughing so hard that they didn't notice Jack come back into the Green Room. Under the watchful eye of one of the stagehands, they were playing with one of the three identical motorised crocodiles from *Peter Pan*. Three were required so the production could always have one on stage at any time, one in reserve and one in the workshop being mended. Tom and Cosmo were running across the Green Room and Eel was operating the remote control and making the crocodile chase them, its jaws snapping furiously. It was terrifyingly realistic and the tick-tock noise it made when it moved was rather ominous.

"Can you stop the noise just for a moment, kids?" asked Jack. "I need to think."

Eel dropped the remote control and snuggled up next to Jack on the sofa. Cosmo began showing Tom a new computer game. He could still be really arrogant and rude, but Tom had begun to realise that a great deal of Cosmo's bluster was simply to disguise his lack of confidence. When he dropped the front, he could be rather nice, and it was showing in his performance as Peter. Alicia's hard work with him was beginning to pay off as he displayed the right mixture of cockiness and vulnerability on stage.

"Is everything all right, Dad? You look really worried," said Eel.

"I am," replied Jack. "One of the wires for the flying has come loose again. It keeps happening, and I don't understand it. I check it and it's fine, and then when I go back half an hour later, it's loose again. It's as if it's taken on a life of its own." It was not the first incident with the flying apparatus. Only a few days before, when Cosi had been lowered from the air, the stagehand had discovered that her safety harness had been unclipped. If she had fallen, it could have been disastrous and when Jasper had found out about it, he had shouted at Jack and even waved his hook at him.

"She could have been killed," he roared, and Cosi looked really frightened, as if she had only just realised how serious it all was.

Jack had held an investigation, but the stagehand concerned, Gary, had sworn blind that he had done up the clip and Jack was certain the man was telling the truth. He had written it in the incident book and instigated a new system of extra checks whenever any of the children were flying. He'd been shaken by what had happened and was being doubly vigilant. And now this latest episode with the wire was beginning to make him doubt himself.

At that moment Olivia and Cosi walked into the Green Room. Jack, Eel and Tom stared at them, amazed. They had come straight from wardrobe and they were wearing identical Edwardian-style white nighties and each had a blue bow in her hair. Olivia's straight hair had been ringletted so it looked just the same as Cosi's.

"Wow," said Tom. "That is seriously spooky."

"You do look amazingly alike," said Jack.

"I can hardly tell the difference," said

Cosmo.

"Oh, you know," said Cosi breezily. "She's the one who can fly and act, and I'm the one who can't."

"Don't be silly, Cosi," said Olivia. "You're really improving fast." She saw that Jack was looking tired. She knew it meant that he was worrying about something. "Are you all right, Dad?"

He smiled at her and the years fell away from his handsome face. "Fine. It's just another hiccup with the flying apparatus. I'm beginning to think it's jinxed. One of the wires keeps loosening when it shouldn't. I can't work out why it keeps happening."

"Does it matter?"

"Not by itself. There are plenty of other inbuilt safety precautions. Although one of you children could get a nasty bump if it wasn't totally tight."

"But nobody would get killed or really badly hurt, would they?" asked Cosi anxiously. "They might just get a bit shaken up and bruised? Like that actress who played Peter Pan who the stagehands used like a wrecking ball?"

Jack laughed. "So you've heard that story,

137

have you? There's nothing for you to worry about, Cosi. Remember I showed you how it all works and which wires do what. You won't be dropped, I promise, and you won't come to any harm, not on my watch. You're safe as houses."

At that moment, Jon walked into the room. He did a double take when he saw Olivia and Cosi.

"That's amazing! Wardrobe and make-up have done a fantastic job. I'd have to look hard to tell you two apart. The audience is never going to guess that it's not you doing all the flying, Cosi." He looked at Jack. "Shall we practise the swap now? Is everything ready?"

"Yes, I've just checked all the equipment, it's all in order and we're ready to go."

"OK. Around ten minutes until everyone on stage. I'll put a two-minute call out for you."

"I'll be flying first out the Darling nursery window and then Livy will take over from me, won't she?" asked Cosi, sounding anxious.

"Yes," said Jon. He peered into Cosi's pale face. "There's absolutely nothing to be worried about, you know. It's all under control. I promise."

Cosi smiled wanly and hurried away,

while everyone else waited in the Green Room for Jon's call to assemble in the wings.

But when they trooped on stage, Jon changed his mind. Cosi seemed to be so very nervous that he decided to put Olivia up first, just to give Cosi some confidence.

"Actually, let's get Livy to play the scene when Wendy flies into Never Land and gets shot down by the Lost Boys," said Jon.

"But you said I was flying first," said Cosi, looking stricken. "Please let me fly first."

Jon was so surprised to hear Cosima volunteering to fly that he decided to do what she wanted, but then Jasper Wood snarled, "Zip it, Cosi. Watch and learn from that other kid. She actually knows what she's doing."

Jasper, who had made no connection between the girl he'd insulted over supper at the Savoy and the one employed as his daughter's flying double, had never bothered to learn Olivia's name, or the names of any of the other children. He kept calling Tom "that boy". He nodded at Jon. "Don't listen to my daughter. Do what you want to do, just don't spend all day doing it. I don't want to be here at midnight."

Jon bit back a reply and nodded at Olivia.

"Up you go, Livy. Use Cosi's harness; it's all set up." Cosima went and sat in the front stalls, chewing her front lip furiously.

"Positions, please," called Jon. He nodded to the children playing the Lost Boys. "From 'Did you see the pirates?', please."

"Did you see the pirates?" asked Jonah Nicholls, who was playing the First Twin.

"No," said Dom Carrick, who played Nibs, "but I saw a wonderfuller thing. I saw the loveliest great white bird. It is flying this way. It looks so weary, and as it flies it moans 'Poor Wendy'."

"I remember now, there are birds called Wendies," said another of the Lost Boys as Olivia appeared framed against a sky-blue backdrop, drooping convincingly as if she'd flown thousands of miles through the night and straight on until morning.

"There's Tinkerbell. She says that Peter wants us to shoot the Wendy bird," cried Tootles. He got out his bow and arrow, aimed it at Olivia and let the arrow fly. It hit her and as it did Olivia felt herself slip. The wire jerked sharply and instead of dropping straight to the floor in the controlled manner she was meant to, she was swung violently against the scenery. The noise her head made as it hit the surround made all the adults wince. There were shouts from the stagehands who rushed to help her, but Ali, the little boy playing Slightly, didn't realise that something had gone badly wrong and went ahead and delivered his line. "That's no bird. It must be a lady," he shouted.

"And I've killed her," cried Cosima as she clambered on to the stage. She kneeled by Olivia, who was out cold. "Oh, Livy, Livy, please wake up. Please don't be dead."

Jack had rushed on to the stage from the wings. He was as white as a ghost. "Someone call an ambulance," he shouted.

Olivia began to stir.

"We'll take you to hospital, Liv darling," said Jack, holding her hand and stroking it gently.

"No!" protested a confused-sounding Olivia very crossly. "I'm not Liv Darling. I'm Wendy Darling and I want to see the mermaids. Peter promised that he'd show me the mermaids."

Chapter Fifteen

Olivia was sitting up in bed in exactly the same room she'd been in after she'd fallen off the trapeze the previous term.

"You do seem to lead an exceptionally dangerous life," said the ward sister, tutting loudly. "It's lovely to see you again, Olivia, but I do wish you'd stop hitting your head. It's not good for it. At least it's only a touch of concussion this time. We'll have you out and about again tomorrow but the doctor wants you to stay in overnight so we can keep an eye on you." She turned to Jack. "Mr Marvell, could I have a word, please?"

"She's going to tell him off. She's got a really stern look in her eye," whispered Olivia as Jack followed the ward sister looking like a naughty boy being sent to the head teacher.

"I think she's only pretending to be stern, I bet she really fancies him," said Eel, swinging her feet. "She blushes every time he speaks to her. So does Chloe Bonar. She makes eyes at him but I don't think he's noticed." She looked hard at Olivia. "Do you think Dad might get married again one day? If he did, we'd have a new mother."

"Nobody could ever replace Mum," said Olivia firmly. "Certainly not Chloe Bonar."

"I can't really remember Mum," said Eel sadly. "I wish I could; she looks so beautiful in Gran's painting and Dad's photos. And so young."

"She was young; she was only twenty-five when she died," said Olivia. Then she added thoughtfully, "She'll always be twenty-five. Dad and you and me, we get older every day, but she always stays the same. Frozen in time. A bit like Peter Pan, the boy who never grows up." She shivered. "One day we'll both be older than she was when she died. Isn't that a strange thought?" She suddenly felt incredibly sad.

"Are you sure you're all right, Livy? You don't think you're still Wendy, do you?"

Olivia laughed. "I was just a bit confused after I'd bumped my head, that's all."

"You weren't the only one. Tom says Cosi got quite hysterical and insisted that it was all her fault that you'd been hurt. She wouldn't stop crying even when the paramedics said you were going to be fine."

"And I am fine. It's nobody's fault."

"Yes, it is," said Jack, walking back into the room. "It's my fault. I know everyone else thinks so too. Even the ward sister. She thinks I'm a negligent father for allowing you to do such dangerous things. Maybe she's right. I've certainly been negligent over this. I am in charge of flying, after all. I'm sorry, Liv. I've let you down." He sighed. "I just don't understand what went wrong. I checked that wire over and over." His mobile bleeped.

"What's wrong, Dad?" asked Olivia, seeing his face fall as he read the message.

"It's Jon. He and Jasper and the producers want a meeting. If you're all right for a while I'd better go to the theatre and face the music. I'll come straight back."

The ward sister came in saying that Olivia needed to rest, so after much hugging and

144

kissing Jack and Eel went off together. Olivia hated to see her dad look so crushed.

She wasn't sure how long she dozed. But she was dreaming of lagoons and pirates, and Jasper Wood dressed as Captain Hook making her walk the plank off the edge of the stage and into the auditorium where a giant ticking crocodile was waiting for her in the orchestra pit with its jaws wide open, when she heard the door open. She looked up drowsily.

"Hello, Livy," said Katie Wilkes-Cox. She had a huge envelope under her arm.

"Katie?" said Olivia, surprised. "How did you know I was here?"

"I knew you were involved with *Peter Pan* so I went to the theatre and met Tom coming out the stage door. He told me, rather reluctantly, that there had been an accident and you were in here. He clearly wanted to protect you, and I don't really blame him." She sighed. "Are you all right?"

"Just a little bang to the head," said Olivia, shifting herself upright. "Thanks for not giving me away the other night. I'm really grateful."

Katie smiled. "I would've been in touch before but Dad's been keeping a close eye on me. Nice work, unplugging all the equipment." Olivia grinned. "Dad was completely furious. He couldn't work out how somebody had got in and out of the building through a locked door. He'd put on a padlock when we were leaving. He thought it must be some particularly ingenious hooligans or a ghost. But of course he couldn't complain to the police because they'd want to know what he was using the sound equipment for and he could hardly admit that he was trying to harass Miss Swan into selling the school to him at a cut price. Has it been quieter?"

"Yes, much," said Olivia. "But I don't think he's given up. Gran sometimes still looks really frightened. I don't think the threatening phone calls have stopped."

"They won't. Dad'll never give up," said Katie. "And I'm afraid the noise will be starting again soon because he's actually going to start work converting the building into luxury flats for real. What happened with the equipment really put the wind up him and he's in a real hurry to get the job done. That means he'll be more determined than ever to try and make Miss Swan sell, and as quickly as possible because he'll want to work on both buildings at the same time. It'll be much cheaper for him that way."

Olivia sighed.

"I wish there was something we could do to stop him," she said. "I was going to talk to Dad about it, but he's got enough on his plate. But, Katie, why are you here?"

"I've found out something I think you should know. I'm afraid I didn't bring you any grapes but I did bring you a present of sorts."

"What is it?" asked Olivia.

Katie sat down in the chair next to Olivia's bed, took some papers out of the envelope and spread them out over the blanket. Olivia stared at them but they didn't make much sense to her.

"Is it some kind of floor plan?" she asked.

"Yes," said Katie triumphantly. "Of the derelict building. And look at this!" She pointed to where the plan covered the land between the back of the Swan and the river. "Can you spot what's missing?" Olivia stared at the plans till her brain hurt, then shook her head.

"The trees!" said Katie. "Somehow Dad's managed to get permission to cut down all those beautiful trees so that the people who buy his flats have a river view. Apparently being able to see the river immediately adds thousands of pounds to the price of each flat. The trees wouldn't be a problem for the penthouse suites at the top, but everyone in the flats below would have their view blocked. You can't sell a river-view flat where there's no view of the river."

"But some of those trees have been there for over two hundred years! It would be vandalism to cut them down."

"Exactly," said Katie. "And if you feel like that, other people will too, I'm sure. Nobody is going to get upset about someone building luxury flats, but they will get upset about the trees being destroyed for no reason but profit. Provided they get to hear about it before he's done the deed. We need to save the trees because it's the trees that'll save the Swan."

"Brilliant! You're so clever," said Olivia, throwing her arms around Katie, who looked very surprised and pleased.

"Yes, well, I've always been clever," she said ruefully. "I've just not always been very nice."

"We'll have to start a campaign."

"You'll have to do that, Livy. I can't be seen to be involved. I've got to keep Dad trusting me so I can get you all the information you need.

I've done my bit for the time being; the rest is up to you and whoever you can get to help. You've got great friends like Tom and Aeysha and Georgia. I know they won't let you down."

Katie's phone bleeped. She looked at the message. "That's Dad, wondering where I am. I've got to go." She gathered up the plans and stuffed them back into the envelope.

A few minutes after she'd gone, the door opened again and Cosi appeared holding a very large plant.

"Oh, Livy, I'm so sorry. Are you feeling better?" she said.

"I'm fine, just fine," said Olivia soothingly. "Stop worrying, Cosi."

"But I feel so awful. It should have been me who was up there, not you."

"Lucky it was me. I'm much more experienced. If it had been you, you might have done yourself some serious harm."

"I really want to make it up to you."

"Really, Cosi, you've nothing to make up to me," said Olivia, who was beginning to feel a bit irritated by Cosi's abject apologies. "Though you could do me a favour?"

"Anything, Livy!"

"Well," said Olivia. "You know you're always talking about how we must look after the trees and how much you want to stop talking about the environment and start doing something about it instead?"

Cosi nodded.

"Well, I've got the perfect opportunity for you," said Olivia, and she started to explain to Cosi about Mr Wilkes-Cox's plan to cut down the trees.

Cosi listened in horrified silence, before crying, "We must stop him!"

"We must, and we'll be saving the Swan at the same time."

Cosi lifted her chin. "Then let's get started immediately."

Chapter Sixteen

A meeting was taking place in the Green Room of the Imperial Theatre. The atmosphere was tense.

"It's not the first time there's been a problem with the flying, Jack," said Jon. "There was the problem with Cosima's safety harness."

"Yes, it's all here," said Jack, pointing to the incident book. "I've kept meticulous notes about everything that's happened. I haven't hidden anything."

Jon sighed. Jack had been so scrupulous about recording every tiny little incident, from a frayed rope to a broken weight or counterweight, that there was now an entire dossier that could be used against him.

Jasper Wood certainly seemed to be very

keen to do just that. "I can't believe this has happened," he said. "What kind of two-bit operation are you running here, Jon? It could have been Cosima who was up there. She might have been killed! And you'd have been to blame, Jack Marvell. I've heard about you and your stunts. You're a reckless madman. I don't care if you want to put your own life in danger but you're not putting my daughter's life on the line. She's too valuable to me."

"And you think Liv isn't precious to me?" asked Jack between gritted teeth. "I think you're forgetting that it was my daughter who was up there and it's Liv who's now lying in a hospital bed. I'd never do anything to put her at risk, or any other child either. It doesn't matter whose daughter or son it is. Don't you understand how wretched I feel about the whole thing?"

"I could sue you for negligence," said Jasper nastily.

"You could," said Jack. "But you'd be wasting your money because I haven't got any. In any case, Cosima is fine; she hasn't come to any harm. Neither have you or Cosmo. The only person who's been hurt is Liv, and she's already insisting that she'll be back at rehearsals the day after tomorrow."

"It's not good enough," said Jasper.

"No," said Jack. "It's not, and that's why I won't be back at rehearsals myself. I'm resigning. It's the only honourable thing to do. If I can't keep the children safe then somebody who can must take over the flying operation." He stood up and pressed a letter into Jon's hand.

"Jack, let's talk about this—" said Jon.

But Jasper cut him off. "Of course he has to resign, otherwise he would have had to be fired. We can't have a reckless daredevil like him looking after something like this. He's a menace." And with that, Jasper stormed dramatically from the room.

"I'm sorry, Jack," said Jon, clapping him on the shoulder.

"So am I," said Jack. "But maybe he's right. Maybe I *am* too reckless for this kind of work. After all, I was nearly responsible for killing my own daughter."

"No," said Olivia tearfully. "I won't do it! If you can resign, I'll resign too."

"Liv, chick, it's not the same," said Jack, stroking her cheek. "If I hadn't resigned I'd have been sacked. Jasper doesn't want me anywhere near the production or his kids."

"Well, I don't want to be anywhere near him," said Olivia passionately. "They'll have to find somebody else to double for Cosi in the flying scenes. I'm not going to do it, not when they've done this to you, Dad." She felt outraged on his behalf. She knew that lots of people thought Jack must be a daredevil who loved to take outlandish risks, but in reality all his stunts and walks were meticulously planned. Since she had been little and had started to walk the wire he had drummed into her the importance of always assessing the situation and the skills needed to deal with it. "I'm not in the business of risk taking, but of risk avoidance, and you should be too," he had once told her after she had been showing off on the wire one day when she was only eight and fallen. She only avoided hurting herself and some of the other circus people standing below through sheer luck.

Olivia knew that people were talking about Jack. There was intense interest surrounding every aspect of *Peter Pan*, and already lots of gossip was spreading on the Internet. What was going on in rehearsals, could the twins actually act, and might Jasper Wood be the greatest Captain Hook ever? After a statement had been put out by the theatre saying that Jack was leaving the production "by mutual consent", there had been some snide little diary items in the press and one paper had run a story with the headline "Not so Marvellous Now", calling Jack a "fallen hero" and saying he'd been sacked for almost killing the Wood twins. The thought of people thinking badly of her dad pierced Olivia's heart. It made her hate the people responsible, and instead Jack was asking her to carry on working with them as if nothing had happened. She couldn't understand how he could be so forgiving, and Alicia didn't help when she tried very gently to explain that Jack had signed a contract on Olivia's behalf and it would be unprofessional of her to break it.

"That's all you ever worry about, Gran – being professional!" shouted Olivia. "I don't want to be professional, I want to scream and shout and behave very badly, because they've all behaved very badly to my dad."

Alicia bit her lip. There had been an accident and Jack had taken full responsibility for it. He clearly didn't see himself as blameless. But there was a horrible little voice in her head that was questioning whether it had been an accident at all. The threatening phone calls hadn't stopped, and the voice at the other end of the phone seemed alarmingly well informed about Alicia's family's involvement in *Peter Pan*. Alicia would do anything to keep them safe, and she was beginning to think that if that meant signing the Swan away, then that's what she would do.

In the end it was Jack who persuaded Olivia to return. He was going to take over Pablo's teaching at the Swan for a few weeks while Pablo took over his old job on *Peter Pan*.

"I came to an agreement with Jon, and he cleared it with the producers without involving Jasper. It means I can keep an eye on things from a distance but Pablo will need all the help he can get. So you really would be helping me in the best way possible if you returned, because perhaps you and Pablo will find out what went wrong with the flying system and help clear my name."

There was another reason too. On the morning she had returned from the hospital Olivia had picked up Alicia's mobile because it kept on ringing and her grandmother was nowhere to be seen.

She was about to ask if she could take a message when a voice said, "Sell up or you'll be sorry. You time is running out." Then the phone went dead.

Straightaway her own phone rang. It was Cosi.

"I'm so sorry about Jack, Livy. I feel so bad. Cosmo and I are furious with Dad. But when are you coming back? Tom and I have been making plans about how to stop the trees being cut down and save the Swan. He's got Georgia and Aeysha involved too, and Eel, and all the Swan kids in the cast. Even Cosmo is fired up. We need you. We can't do it without you."

Chapter Seventeen

Alicia looked out of her office window, which gave her a good view of the back of the Swan. It was lunchtime, and almost the entire school appeared to be having some kind of meeting by the trees near the river. What were they doing? She was really intrigued. She could see that Olivia, Tom, Aeysha and Cosmo were busy handing out something that looked like bundles of leaflets to the other children. Some of the older pupils such as Kasha and Jazz were helping them. What on earth was going on?

Even more astonishingly, she could see that Cosi was standing on an upturned recycling box and was talking to the crowd passionately. She kept pointing at the derelict building and then at the trees. Alicia couldn't hear what Cosi was saying but she didn't need to: it was clear from her body language and the way she was moving her hands that her speech was making a real impression on all the other children. She had them in the palm of her hand.

Alicia frowned and wished Cosi could act with the same conviction when she was playing Wendy. If she could keep the Swan children enraptured just by talking to them, she could certainly do the same with an audience in the theatre. But so far there was no sign of it.

The day after tomorrow would bring the first preview of *Peter Pan*. Everyone was worried about Cosi, who got more and more nervous as her debut in front of a paying audience approached. She had actually got to grips with the dialogue now and there were moments when she was more than competent as Wendy, particularly in her scenes with the Lost Boys, although whenever she had to act anywhere in the vicinity of her dad she tended to become flustered. But instead of gaining confidence, she seemed to be losing it. There had even been a couple of rehearsals recently when either Olivia or Cosi's understudy, a girl called Petal who was at another stage school, had had to take over.

Olivia, thought Alicia, was much the best of all of them. She would have taken great delight in watching her granddaughter blossom as an actor, if she wasn't so concerned about how Cosi was going to cope when the previews began. At least Cosmo was doing much better. He really enjoyed having Tom around, and Alicia had worked hard with him on his accent. There were times, particularly when she had seen him playing opposite Olivia, when he really captured all the heartless charm of Peter Pan. She reckoned that by the time press night arrived, Cosmo would have the measure of Peter and get good reviews. She also had to admit that although she didn't like him and deplored the careless way he treated his children, Jasper Wood was very good too. Perhaps a little too much the pantomime villain for her taste but she was certain *Peter Pan* was going to revive his career. He was very charismatic in a shivery sort of way.

She glanced again out of the window. Cosi had clearly reached the climax of her speech. She raised her arm with a gesture that suggested she was rousing them to action and all the children cheered and stamped. Cosi was clearly an inspiring public speaker. As she watched the children start to disperse, Alicia wondered what it was that had made Cosi feel so impassioned. But she didn't have too long to think about it because Sebastian Shaw was knocking on her office door.

"I think you'd better come and see this, Alicia." He led her down the stairs and out into the street. Several bulldozers and mechanical diggers were being driven up the road and on to the site next door.

"I don't know what all that noise was about before," he said, "but I think the real disruption to the Swan is about to begin."

It was very late that night. It was dark and nobody was around outside the back of the Imperial Theatre, except for Jack and Olivia, who were walking quietly towards the scenery dock.

"What are we doing here, Liv?" whispered Jack. "I feel as if I'm in some kind of thriller movie creeping around in the dark like this. We should be in bed. It's a big day for you tomorrow. It's the first preview."

"Trust me," Olivia whispered back.

"I do, Liv, chick," he said and squeezed her hand. Olivia got out her mobile and pressed a button.

"We're here," she whispered into it and immediately ended the call. For a few seconds there was silence but for the yowl of a cat and the sound of a car passing, and then the scene-dock door creaked. This opened on to the vast backstage and was the route by which scenery was brought in and out of the theatre. It slid open a few centimetres and Pablo beckoned them in, closing the door behind them.

"What's this all about? Why all the cloak and dagger stuff?" asked Jack.

"We think it's not good if you are seen here at the theatre, Jack," explained Pablo. "That Jasper, he is a rude bully who wouldn't like you being here."

"But you need to be here, Dad," said Olivia, "because Pablo's got something to show you."

"What is it?" asked Jack.

"This," said Pablo, holding up two pieces of rope.

Jack looked at the rope and whistled. "This didn't fray or break, it's been cut clean in two."

Pablo nodded.

"Pablo says it couldn't have been an accident. It's been done deliberately," said Olivia.

"It is not the first time, Jack," said Pablo. "Like you, I find that wires I have already checked are mysteriously coming loose. At first I thought it was bad luck and then I thought it was me. I thought I was, how do you say it. . .?"

"Incompetent," said Jack.

"That's right. Incompetent."

"That's what I decided I was," said Jack sadly. "I came to the conclusion that I just wasn't up to the job."

"No, Dad. You *are* up to the job and so is Pablo. But somebody really doesn't want the flying system to work."

"Sabotage!" said Jack.

Pablo and Olivia nodded. "Yes, I'm very certain," said Pablo.

"The cut rope certainly points that way," said Jack. He frowned. "But who would do such a thing? It's an insanely dangerous thing to do. Somebody could be killed."

"That's why we've got to find out who's responsible and stop them," said Olivia.

"And that's why I'm keeping a twenty-four-hour watch on the rigging," said Pablo. "I want to know who is doing this and why."

Pablo let Jack and Olivia out of the theatre and they walked off down the road. They hadn't gone far when Olivia's mobile rang.

"Livy? It's Katie. I can't talk for long. Tomorrow. Saturday. Twelve noon. That's when he's going to start to cut the trees down. You need to mobilise everyone. Good luck."

"Thanks," said Olivia.

Her dad looked at her in surprise. "Who was that ringing you at almost midnight?" he asked.

"An unexpectedly good friend," said Olivia with a grin as she started texting furiously, and Jack knew not to press her further. He trusted Olivia and knew she'd tell him when she was ready.

They hadn't gone very far when Olivia suddenly asked, "Are you doing anything tomorrow morning, Dad?"

"Why? What would you like me to do?"

"I think we're going to need some adult help," said Olivia, and she told Jack at top speed about Alicia's sinister phone calls, and the threat to the Swan, and about Mr Wilkes-

Cox's determination to cut down the trees, and all the while she talked she continued to write and send messages.

Chapter Eighteen

Mr Wilkes-Cox and Bill Jukes stared in astonishment at the sight in front of them. It was Saturday morning and when they had arrived at the site a couple of hours ago there had been nobody around down by the river. It was a blustery day, not the kind of weather for walkers or families to be out and about in. They were delighted; it would mean fewer people to see what they were up to, and once the deed was done there would be nothing anybody could do about it. The trees would be gone.

"It'll be easy," said Bill Jukes. "We'll get in there and get the trees down. It should only take an hour or two with all this equipment. You've got plenty of workmen to do the job?"

"Ten of the best," said Mr Wilkes-Cox. "I'm

paying them handsomely to ask no questions and just get on with it as quickly and efficiently as possible. It'll all be over and done with in time for a late lunch. Provided we don't run into any problems."

"We won't," said Bill confidently. "Nobody knows what we're going to do, and by the time they cotton on it'll be too late. The trees will be gone and the new flats will have a beautiful and – for us – very profitable view of the river."

"But what if someone challenges us?" asked Mr Wilkes-Cox.

"We show them this piece of paper that says it's all signed, sealed and approved and that you've got permission to cut the trees down. And you have. I signed the form myself. It's all official; nobody can dispute it. It's watertight." Bill Jukes chuckled. "We just don't want people asking questions in case they get really interested in the tender process. If they do it could come out that it wasn't legal and that Alicia Swan put in a higher bid and should have got the building, instead of me practically giving it away to you. You know what these Save the Earth types are like; they like a cause to rally around. Once the trees are gone it'll be plain sailing. So if anyone asks, I'm simply here to make sure the whole operation goes smoothly. And it will, after that very nice back-hander you gave me. It's going to pay for a holiday villa in Spain."

Initially it looked as if he was right and everything would go smoothly. The workmen had moved all the equipment into place and everything was set to go. But then they had demanded a tea break. Nobody liked Mr Wilkes-Cox's blustering, bullying tone. They had sensed that they were involved in something underhand and shady, and they decided to play it for all it was worth. They all disappeared to the café across the road, saying they'd be back in twenty minutes. After a minute or two, Bill Jukes and Mr Wilkes-Cox had joined them as it had started to spit with rain.

Twenty-five minutes later, when nobody had moved, Mr Wilkes-Cox looked at his watch pointedly and announced it was time to make a start. "Or I'll dock your money. I'm not paying you to sit around in cafés," he'd said.

The sun had come out and the wind had dropped. They'd all trooped out of the café and back across the road. They heard something before they saw it. It was the distant sound of music and someone drumming, and it became louder and louder as they drew nearer. They hurried down the side of the derelict building and were stopped dead in their tracks by the sight that met their eyes. A look of fury crossed Mr Wilkes-Cox's face.

A couple of hundred people, most of them children, had surrounded the trees. There were mothers with buggies, and lots of people dancing to Kasha Kasparian's band. A number of small children were climbing the trees and playing pirates. There was bunting threaded through the top branches of the trees and a banner had been draped between two of the oldest and most beautiful ones saying: "Save Our Trees. Put the Planet before Profit." Another banner read: "Swans in Solidarity with Trees (and Polar Bears)." A third read: "Any Fool Can Destroy Trees." Jack had just finished fixing up a zip-wire and a queue of children had already formed to use it, and he was helping them down with the aid of some of the older Swans.

Bill Jukes gulped. Mr Wilkes-Cox turned a dangerous shade of red. He marched towards the trees.

"Oi," he shouted. "Get out of the way.

We've got a job to do." Nobody took a blind bit of notice; few people even heard him. Mr Wilkes-Cox turned an unattractive puce colour.

"Clear off," he yelled and he ran towards the band and kicked over the drums. The crowd became ominously quiet and everyone turned and stared at him.

"What a baby!" said a woman, making the people around her grin.

"My six-year-old has better manners," said another woman, and everyone laughed. Aeysha and Georgia clapped and cheered. By now Mr Wilkes-Cox was a ghastly purple.

"Your six-year-old hasn't got a piece of paper entitling him to cut down these trees," Mr Wilkes-Cox shouted into her face.

"He wouldn't want to cut them down. Only an idiot would do that. They're beautiful," said the woman.

"They are," said Jack, moving up very close to Mr Wilkes-Cox. "You clearly don't understand something a six-year-old would find simple: we don't inherit the earth from our ancestors, we borrow it from our children." Everyone cheered.

Cosi marched right up to Mr Wilkes-Cox and wagged her finger in his face. "What makes you think you've got the right to cut down my future and the future of all the children here?"

"I don't care about your future, or your children's children's future. It's not my concern. I won't be around to see it," said Mr Wilkes-Cox, striding towards one of the diggers. "I've got a right to cut down these trees, I've got the paper and the official stamp to prove it, and I'm going to start right now."

"Over my dead body," said Cosi, sitting down in front of the digger just a few metres from its toothy jaws.

"And mine," said Kasha, sitting down next to her. He was joined by his friend, Jazz, who was joined by Kylie Morris. They linked arms with Olivia, Georgia and the other Swans. Tom got out his phone and began filming the scene. A couple of other people did the same. Kasha and Jazz began tweeting.

"And mine and my children's," said a woman, taking her place with a baby in her arms. Bill Jukes was beginning to look worried. He realised that the situation was getting out of control. He didn't want anything to draw attention to him or his signature on that piece of paper, and he was worried about the people filming on their mobile phones. If it was discovered that he had taken a bribe from a property developer he'd go to prison. This wasn't working out quite as he'd hoped it would. Several of the workmen were looking unhappy too.

"We didn't come here to hurt anyone," one of them muttered.

"I thought we were just cutting down a few trees," said another. "Nobody said anything about a load of kids. I'm off." He turned and walked away and the others followed. Furious, Mr Wilkes-Cox leapt into the cab of a digger and turned the ignition. The machine roared into life and edged menacingly forwards.

"This isn't a good idea," shouted Bill Jukes. But Mr Wilkes-Cox ignored him and still the digger edged forwards. The seated crowd began to murmur anxiously, and some of the children burst into tears as the digger crept forwards very slowly towards the people sitting in the front row. Cosi saw what was happening and she started to walk towards the moving digger.

"Cosi!" cried Olivia. Somebody screamed. Mr Wilkes-Cox panicked and fumblingly applied the brake. Cosi stood her ground. She didn't even step back and the digger stopped just a few centimetres from her toes. Cosi leaned forward against the front of it with her arms folded as if it was the most natural place in the world to stop for a rest. The only way Mr Wilkes-Cox could move the digger forward was by running her over. Kasha was tweeting furiously.

"Get out of my way!" roared Mr Wilkes-Cox. But Cosi just stared him squarely in the eye and didn't budge. Mr Wilkes-Cox swung down from the cab and moved round towards Cosi, looking as if he might take a swing at her. Cosi didn't flinch, but Jack stepped in between them. Bill Jukes put a restraining hand on Mr Wilkes-Cox's shoulder, and at that moment there came a cry of "Doodle doo, cock a doodle doo" from the very top of the tallest tree. It was a most eerie sound. "Doodle doo, cock a doodle doo," it came again, and as it did a crocodile appeared from the bank of the river behind the trees and moved very fast across the ground straight towards Bill Jukes and Mr Wilkes-Cox. Its monstrous jaws were opening and closing as if it was extremely hungry and urgently in need of a large snack.

A look of horror crossed the men's faces as

the crocodile ignored the rest of the crowd and zoomed straight towards them, its giant mouth wide open. The crocodile looked incredibly realistic, and Bill Jukes and Mr Wilkes-Cox were so terrified that they didn't notice the odd tick-tock noise that came from its belly, but simply turned on their heels and ran. The crocodile followed close behind them, snapping at their feet. The crowd laughed and clapped, and up at the top of the tree, Cosmo, Tom and Aeysha continued to doodle-doo delightedly. People crowded around Cosi before Kasha and his friends hoisted her on to their shoulders with a big cheer, although Cosi looked terrified to be so far off the ground. Olivia went over to Jack and hugged him.

"Aren't you pleased that you agreed to go back to the theatre last night to get the crocodile?"

Jack grinned. "It was an inspired idea. I'll never forget the look on Wilkes-Cox's face."

Eel came rushing over to give the remote control back to Jack. "That was such fun!" she said.

"It was," said Olivia. Kasha lowered Cosi to the ground and Olivia squeezed her hand. "You were so brave, Cosi. You saved the trees.

And the Swan."

"You showed immense courage," added Jack. "I'm really proud of you, Cosi."

For a moment Cosi looked as if she was going to cry, and she began to speak. "I've been such a coward, I need to tell—" but she was cut off by Cosmo sweeping her up in a massive bear hug and the cheer that went up among the crowd drowned her out anyway. "We saved the trees! We saved the trees!"

"We did," said Jack quietly. "But for how long?"

"You think they'll be back?" asked Georgia.

"I know they will," said Jack. "Mr Wilkes-Cox won't give up that easily. It's rather lucky I've unexpectedly got a lot of time on my hands."

"What do you mean?" asked Eel.

"I can conduct my lessons out here. We'll fix up a swing and a high-wire between the trees," said Jack. "I'm going to live in the trees."

"Wow," said Eel. "Can I live in the trees too?"

"No, you cannot, Eel Marvell," said Alicia, who had just returned from shopping and come to investigate. "What on earth is going on here? I've just seen two men, one who seemed to be

Katie Wilkes-Cox's dad, running down the road looking as if they were being pursued by all the devils in hell."

"Not devils, Gran. It was just a crocodile," said Eel, as if this was a perfectly normal thing to happen to anyone in London on a Saturday morning. The band struck up again, Kasha began to sing and the crowd started to dance.

"I think you'd better get the croc back to Pablo at the theatre before anyone realises it's missing," said Jack. "Then I'm going to need some help here. Alicia, I'm going to need – among other things – flour. Lots of it. We need to hurry. You and Tom and Cosi and the others need to get to the theatre by late afternoon for the first preview tonight." Only Jack noticed that Cosi looked as if he had just announced her imminent execution.

Chapter Nineteen

Alicia and Jack were sitting in the lower branches of a large tree drinking tea out of a Thermos. It was late afternoon. Olivia and the others had helped bring him bits of wood and rope from the Swan as well as several hoses and blankets and a sleeping bag before they had gone to the theatre. Jack had been flat out all afternoon and he'd just finished fixing up some wires so he could move between the trees quickly and easily. He'd also borrowed two of Pablo's trapezes and fixed them to the branches. Some children and their parents were still playing on the zip-wire, and Kylie Morris and her mum had just left after bringing Jack a chocolate cake.

"Have a slice, Alicia, it's delicious. If I eat all of it, I'll fall out of the tree."

Alicia was rather surprised to find herself sat on a branch. She had thought that her tree-climbing days were long over; her arthritis often made it troublesome for her to even get up and down the stairs. But Jack had helped her, found her a cushion so she could rest her back against another branch without falling, and given her a blanket. And although they were only just a metre or two off the ground, Alicia had found the whole experience unexpectedly exhilarating.

"It takes me right back to my childhood. It must be forty years since I last sat in a tree, Jack," she said. "It's funny, when you're a child you never know that you might be doing something for the very last time. You don't think to yourself, 'This the last time I climb a tree, or dam a stream or walk along that wall on the way to school.' We don't notice adult preoccupations taking over, do we? We feel just the same, but one morning we wake up and we're quite grown up, and it crept up on us while we had our backs turned."

Jack nodded. "It's probably just as well, Alicia, that we don't notice, otherwise we'd spend our childhood constantly saying goodbye to things, like you do when you go on holiday. 'This is the last time I'll have breakfast here and this is the last time I'll sleep in this bed.' If you were always saying goodbye to childhood, you couldn't really live it; you'd be too self-conscious about it."

"It's true," said Alicia. "But inside I still feel as if I'm twelve, not fifty-two. I don't know where the time has gone."

"Alicia," said Jack softly. "I wish you'd told me about the threatening phone calls. I could have done something to help."

"I know you would have done, Jack, but I thought they would eventually just stop when I made it quite clear I wouldn't sell."

"If you get any more we should call the police."

"I rather think I might have had the last one," said Alicia. "It can only be Mr Wilkes-Cox who's behind them, and now he knows what he's up against I think he may give up. But I do wonder whether there might be a connection between the calls and the sabotage at the theatre."

"What an interesting thought," said Jack.

Alicia smiled. "I bet Mr Wilkes-Cox was mortified to have been outwitted by a bunch of children and a mechanical crocodile."

"I'm just worried that it might make him more determined to cut down the trees and get his hands on the Swan. I'm not sure you're right to think this will stop him. He seems like a man who will stop at nothing."

Just then, Eel, Georgia and Aeysha arrived. They were already dressed to go to the first preview of *Peter Pan*.

"Are you really going to sleep here tonight, Dad?" asked Eel enviously.

"Not just tonight. Every night, if necessary. What we need is to get some really good publicity for what's happening here. That's the way to stop it."

"Kasha is putting some of the video clips of Cosi facing the bulldozers on YouTube and tweeting about them," said Georgia.

"That'll help. The trouble is that if Mr Wilkes-Cox has got permission to cut the trees down then there's very little we can do about it. We can protest for all we're worth and mobilise local people, but with the law on his side all we may really be doing is delaying the inevitable. Let's hope that Katie can provide Liv with some more insider information about her dad's activities," said Jack.

"Katie? Kate Wilkes-Cox?" asked Alicia, sounding very surprised.

"Yes," replied Aeysha. "It was only because of Katie telling Liv about the plan to cut down the trees and when it was going to happen that we were able to get everyone out this morning."

"We'd already had a meeting and given out leaflets in the area about the threat to the trees," said Georgia, "but that would all have been useless if Katie hadn't provided precise information about when Mr Wilkes-Cox planned to do the deed."

"I'm astonished," said Alicia. "This can't be the same Katie-Wilkes-Cox who pushed Georgia off the stage in order to steal her starring role in the school concert, who tried to frame Livy for theft and get her sent away from the Swan, and who did everything she could to destroy Livy's friendship with Tom and the others?"

"No," agreed Aeysha. "I don't think it's the same Katie at all. Liv's convinced that she's changed. I think rather than admiring her dad, she's finally seen him for the ruthless weasel he really is."

"That's very brave of her. It must take a lot of courage to stand up for what she thinks is right and go against her own dad. He's always been such a dominant force in her life," said Alicia thoughtfully. She glanced at her watch. "We must go, Jack. I need to get along to the theatre. I just hope that the first preview of *Peter Pan* isn't an awfully big misadventure. I'll make you another Thermos before I go."

Chapter Twenty

Jasper was in his dressing room when the text came through on his smartphone. It was from one of Cosi and Cosmo's ex-minders who he'd packed off back to California. Despite the hefty pay-off Jasper had offered, the man had been furious about the termination of his contract and had warned that the twins would get into all sorts of trouble without him there to keep an eye on them. On the contrary, Jasper thought that the twins had both seemed happier without having somebody constantly on their tail.

Cosmo was turning into a damn fine actor too. He had clearly inherited the family talent. Sometimes when Jasper watched him it made his heart hurt as he was transported back in time to his own childhood when he had sat in the dark of a different auditorium far away in America watching another golden-haired boy play *Peter Pan*. A boy who never grew up. Cosmo wasn't as good. But he showed promise.

Jasper was lost in thoughts of the past, thoughts that he seldom allowed himself. He roused himself in preparation for the preview ahead. He was desperate for it to go well, for a Wood family triumph, but in his heart he knew that Cosi was the weak link. That other girl, the flying double, Octavia, had real talent. He could see it although he'd never admit it. Just as he'd never admit that he really knew her name was Olivia. Olivia Marvell. She had been good for Cosi too, but there was something else about her. She had that indefinable spark that makes you shiver as you watch in the dark, just as he had shivered all those years ago watching that boy play Peter Pan with such careless, heart-breaking grace.

What was he going to do about Cosi? He knew he needed to have more patience with her; he knew that he needed to let her go. But what would she do? She was so wan and listless. She seemed to lack courage but maybe that was because he had made her so afraid of him. It was his fault but he didn't know how to put it right without risking everything that was so precious to him.

Jasper sighed. He supposed he ought to read the goon's text but he guessed it was trouble. The man probably wanted to sue him. He opened it. It simply said, "This will interest you" and underneath was a hyperlink. Curious, Jasper tapped on the link, which took him to YouTube. For a few seconds he couldn't work out what it was that he was watching. He could see lots of trees and people and bulldozers. It was chaotic and noisy. Then he realised that he was watching his own daughter standing in front of a bulldozer to prevent it cutting down the trees. He heard her speak with cool and commanding determination.

Jasper's colour began to rise. He should never have allowed Jon to persuade him to get rid of the minders. Cosi could have been killed. He clenched his fists with fury. He peered more closely at the screen and at Cosi's brave, defiant face as the bulldozer edged inexorably towards her. She didn't even flinch, and there in her bright eyes he suddenly saw it – that indefinable spark. His anger melted away, he felt his throat tighten and he suddenly felt a painful mix of love and pride for his brave daughter.

Olivia was putting the final touches to her make-up. She felt quite nervous, although she knew that she didn't have very much to be nervous about. She loved the flying during *Peter Pan*, and she only had a dozen or so lines to deliver when she was pretending to be Cosi during the flying swaps. She delivered them as much like Cosi did as possible. Everyone had agreed that they looked so alike that nobody would notice, except for Tom who had privately told Georgia and Aeysha that the audience might perceive a sudden improvement in the quality of the acting.

Olivia knew the entire script by heart, having gone over and over it with Cosi and Cosmo to help them learn their lines, and she had filled in on several occasions during rehearsals when Cosi had been absent for some reason. There was part of her that wished that she could get a shot at doing the whole thing in front of an audience, although that was never going to happen because even if Cosi missed a performance it would be Petal, Cosi's understudy, who would go on, not her. She was just the lowly flying double. She didn't even have her name in the programme or get to take a curtain call because nobody connected with the production wanted the audience to know that Cosi wasn't doing all her own flying. Jack had been ticked off for even mentioning her in a little interview he had done when he was still working on the production, and Jon had been really apologetic when he explained that she wouldn't be credited because in a few weeks' time, once the production had opened, everyone hoped that Cosi would eventually be able to handle the flying herself.

Not that Olivia minded about the lack of a credit. Everything she had to do was over by the end of Act III when Wendy, who is stranded with Peter on Marooner's Rock, grabs on to a kite tail that carries her away over the rising water to safety. It meant that by the interval Olivia was free to go, and tonight she wanted to get back to the Swan as soon as possible and check how Jack was doing after taking up residence in the tree. She hoped he wouldn't fall off his perch when he went to sleep.

She finished her make-up, adjusted her blue bow and went off to find Cosi. Poor Cosi had got quieter and quieter as the day had gone on. She was obviously dreading tonight's performance, even though she had got so much better over the last few days. There were scenes in which she was really quite good now. Cosi and Cosmo seemed to have made their peace and Cosmo was really helping his sister as much as he could. Olivia guessed that Tom had had something to do with that. But she knew it would still be a relief to Cosi when the first preview was over. Earlier she had been in the other girl's dressing room and had noticed a series of strokes marked on a large sheet of paper pinned to the wall.

"What's that for?" she'd asked, intrigued.

"Oh, that," said Cosi. "Each stroke represents a performance. There are a hundred and four of them. Every time I've done one I'm going to strike it through."

"But that's what prisoners do in jail to count down the days until they're released," said Olivia, who was rather shocked.

"Well, that's what doing this show feels like to me," said Cosi fiercely. "I feel like I'm imprisoned in a life I don't want to lead. I can't wait until I'm eighteen and I can do what I like. I'll never act again."

Olivia thought how terrible it must be to feel like that and pitied Cosi. Even when she did eventually manage to break free from her dad, she wouldn't be able to get her childhood back. It would be lost forever.

She had a little good-luck present for Cosi. It was a badge with a picture of a polar bear on it with a speech bubble coming out of his mouth saying: "Melting ice is a hot topic for me." Olivia knew that Cosi would love it. She'd been so incredibly brave the way she had stood in front of the digger to save the trees. She had really stood up for something she believed in.

The announcement came over the tannoy that the theatre was now open. Soon it would be filling up with people buying drinks in the bar and looking at their programmes. There were already lots of photographers hanging around outside and it was only the first preview. Olivia decided to go and give her present to Cosi after she'd seen Pablo to check that there hadn't been any further problems with the flying equipment.

"Ah, Livy," he said when he saw her, breaking into a broad grin. "I hear from Tom and Cosmo that the crocodile was a great success and chased the villainous tree-cutters away."

"Yes, it was a case of fighting reptiles with reptiles," said Olivia, smiling. "They got the croc back to you OK?"

Pablo nodded. "Nobody at the theatre ever knew it had gone on a walkabout. But I wonder what the people on the bus it travelled home on thought. Maybe some of them thought it was real."

"Tom and Cosmo bought it back on the bus?"

"Yes. Tom was most unhappy because the driver made him buy a ticket for it. I hear Cosi was very brave this morning, Livy."

"She was amazing," said Olivia. "Everyone was, but particularly Cosi and Jack."

"Jack should be here tonight doing the flying. I'm sorry it is me. He did not deserve what happened to him. His system is perfect."

"Has there been any more sabotage?" whispered Olivia.

Pablo shook his head. "I have not let the rig out of my sight. And now my stomach is growling. Livy, could you watch the equipment for me for a few minutes while I buy a sandwich?"

"Of course, Pablo. No hurry." Pablo went off whistling and Olivia crouched down behind one of the curtains where she'd be hidden from view from anyone who came near. She liked listening to the sounds of the stagehands calling to each other as they made their preparations for the performance. She saw Jon and Jasper Wood, who was dressed as Mr Darling, talking earnestly to each other on top of the pirate ship. Jasper was pointing something out to Jon.

The pirate ship reminded Olivia of a nativity play put on by the Reception class in a school in Cornwall she'd attended. It had been just for a few months while they over-wintered with the circus. Olivia was only little and Eel had just been born. She'd been too shy to take part, but she had helped make the costumes, sticking fruit gums on to the crowns of the three wise men, and trying not to eat too many of them so that there were enough for all three crowns. She had thought that the fruit gums didn't look anything like precious jewels at all. But when she had watched the nativity play from a distance, the crowns looked as if they were studded with rubies and emeralds, and during the performance Olivia had kept tugging Jack's arm and loudly telling baby Eel, who was lying asleep in Toni's arms, "I made them!"

The pirate ship brought the memory back vividly, because it too was a fake constructed largely from wood and gold paint. It didn't even have a deck, and was quite hollow inside with just a few platforms and ladders. But when the *Jolly Roger* sailed into view at the start of Act V, proudly flying the skull and crossbones, it would look just like a real ship to the audience. Even during rehearsal, everyone in the auditorium had clapped when it had first sailed on to the stage, and they all knew it was being operated by a computer and needed an extra shove from behind to get it moving. Suspension of disbelief, wasn't that what it was called? thought Olivia. How amazing that you could sit in a darkened theatre for a few hours and believe the impossible: that children could fly, fairies existed and that Never Land was a real place on the map.

Olivia was snapped out of her thoughts by the sound of someone coming softly towards the flying rig. She guessed it was one of the stagehands just passing by and kept herself hidden. But the footsteps stopped. Olivia peered out from her hiding place, her heart thumping. She was relieved to see that it was only Cosi looking like a little ghost in her white Edwardian night dress. Olivia was about to step out of hiding but something in Cosi's manner made her hesitate. The American girl looked furtively around. Then she reached for one of the ropes, raised her arm and Olivia saw something glinting in her hand.

"Cosi!" cried Olivia, shocked. Cosima swung around, startled to see Olivia appearing from her hiding place.

"I saw Pablo leave . . . I thought . . . I thought nobody would see me. . ." The small, sharp knife in Cosi's hand clattered to the ground between the two of them. For a second both girls looked at it and didn't move. Then Olivia shook her head as if she couldn't believe her eyes and whispered, "It was you! You've been sabotaging the flying rig. Oh, Cosi, how could you?"

Cosi opened her mouth as if to say something but all that came out was a little desperate cry and then she fled, fluttering away like a small, white, wounded bird.

Pablo passed her as he arrived back clutching a coffee and a cheese and tomato panini.

"Is Cosi all right? She looks upset," he

asked. He saw the distress on Olivia's face, and then he noticed the small knife on the ground.

"Livy, what's going on?"

"I can't explain now, Pablo. But you don't need to worry about the rig being sabotaged any more. I know exactly who is responsible." She raced off after Cosi, leaving Pablo staring after her in bewilderment.

Chapter Twenty-One

"How could you?" shouted Olivia. "I can hardly bear to look at you, let alone speak to you. You should be so ashamed of yourself."

"I am," sobbed Cosima. "I hate myself and what I've done."

"You claimed to be my friend but you could have got me killed, and you forced Jack, who has been so kind to you and tried to help you so much, to resign from *Peter Pan* in disgrace. You're despicable. You've betrayed us all. I don't know how I ever thought that you were a real friend."

The two girls were locked in Cosima's dressing room. Olivia had chased up the stairs after Cosi, who had reached her dressing room and tried to slam the door shut in her face. But

Olivia had been too quick for her and had pushed the door open, and once she was through, turned the key in the lock and pocketed it. Cosi had flung herself on to the little bed in the corner and wept uncontrollably. The stage manager's voice came through the tannoy announcing the half and that "The house is now open".

"I don't understand you," said Olivia coldly. "This morning you were *so* brave, and then I discover that you've been doing something that only a coward would do. It's awful. You're awful. I admired you because you really seemed to believe in something and were prepared to stand up and fight for your beliefs. You were amazing when you talked to the school at that meeting and persuaded everybody how important it was to save the trees. We all believed in you because you seemed to believe in something bigger than yourself. But all the time you were just a fake. You may say brave things, do brave things when we're all watching, but when we're not looking you're sneaking around sabotaging other people's hard work and putting their lives in danger."

"I never meant to put anyone's life in danger. If you believe nothing else, please believe that, Livy. I never wanted anyone to get hurt. Not ever," sobbed Cosi.

"So what did you think you were doing?" demanded Olivia.

"I thought the only person risking getting hurt was me," said Cosi in a tiny voice.

"You *wanted* to fall? So that's why you loosened the wires and cut the rope? That's sick," said Olivia, shaking her head.

"No, I didn't want to fall; I was really scared of falling. You know I'm not brave like you and I haven't got a head for heights," said Cosi tearfully. "I just thought that if I got swung around a little bit like that actress did when she played Peter Pan, I'd be able to have a few days off and then either you or Petal could take over and everyone would see how useless I am as Wendy, and I wouldn't have to play her in front of an audience. I swear on my life I never intended for anyone else to get hurt. I specifically got Jack to show me the wires and ropes that worked my harness, so I thought whatever I did it would only be me who could possibly be affected. I never dreamed you'd get hurt or Jack would lose his job because of me. You don't know how much I've wanted to confess and make everything all right again. It's been eating me up inside. I'm so sorry. I really am."

"It's easy to say sorry after the event, when you've been found out," said Olivia scornfully. "But I still don't understand why you'd go to such extreme lengths." The tannoy announced the quarter and Olivia could hear the buzz of the audience as the auditorium began to fill up.

"Because nobody listens to me!" shouted Cosi. "I keep telling everyone that I can't do this. I can just about manage the rehearsals but I can't go out there in front of an audience and be Wendy. But nobody believes me. I've even told you, Livy, but you just tell me that I'm getting better and that it will be all right on the night. Well, the night has come and it's not all right, is it? That's why I tried to cut the rope just now. I'm desperate, Livy. I've been trying to do it all afternoon but Pablo was always there. Then I saw my chance. I was going to cut one of the main ropes so that the entire flying system had to be rerigged and the performance would be cancelled. But you caught me and now you know just how despicable I am."

Olivia said nothing.

Cosi carried on. "I'd would do anything

you asked me to at this minute, even walk into the jaws of a crocodile, apart from one thing. I just can't walk out there on to that stage in a few minutes' time. I just can't do it! Everybody – Dad, Jon, your gran, even Cosmo – they think that I just don't want to do it. That I'm just being a bit flaky. Or that I'm not trying hard enough. They don't understand. I. Can't. Do. It. I'll just freeze."

Despite her fury, Olivia realised that there was something in Cosi's face and tone of voice that made her believe what she was saying. When she thought about it, there had been numerous times when Cosi had told her that she couldn't play Wendy in front of an audience, but like everyone else she hadn't really heard. Maybe she had let her friend down.

She still felt angry with Cosi, particularly for what she had done to Jack, but she also realised that Cosi was a victim of her own powerlessness. She remembered how sad and lonely and angry she had been when she felt that she and Eel had been dumped at the Swan by Jack. She hadn't always behaved well then, and she hadn't been much better last term when she had been upset with Tom and Georgia because they'd chosen to be in *The Sound of Music* rather than *Romeo and Juliet on the High Wire*. Maybe Cosi felt just as she had then, as if everything that happened to her was out of her control. Cosi could speak up for the trees and the polar bears, but she couldn't get her own voice heard. Maybe it *was* possible to be two people at the same time: the selfless Cosi who stood up for injustice and the planet and the cowardly Cosi who had cut the rope.

Cosi was lying very still like a statue, and had gone very pale. Except that unlike a statue Cosi's eyes were dark with fear and her forehead was pricked with sweat. In a flash, Olivia realised that Cosi reminded her of someone: after his accident, Jack had tried to walk the wire again and had become completely paralysed by fear. He couldn't go forwards or backwards. He had frozen. Cosi had said that she would freeze if she had to step out on the stage in front of an audience and Olivia believed her.

She suddenly knew what Cosi was suffering from: stage fright. She had heard Alicia talk about it. Alicia had said that a little bit of stage fright was a good thing, it got the adrenalin pumping and helped an actor give a better performance, but some actors were so overcome with stage fright that they became incapable of performing in front of a live audience, though often they could do TV and film work with no problem. Entire careers had been lost to stage fright or badly blighted by it. Even very famous actors such as Sir Laurence Olivier had suffered from it.

"Beginners, please. Beginners, please," came the call over the tannoy. Cosi gave a squeak of despair and curled up into a little ball. She was shaking all over.

"Get up, Cosi," ordered Olivia.

"I can't, Olivia, I can't. I'm going to be sick."

"You can get up, Cosi, and you must get up," said Olivia firmly.

"You're not listening to me again. I can't do it."

"You don't have to do it. You don't have to play Wendy. I'm going to go out there and play her for you. I'm going to pretend to be you. The rest of the cast will realise, but by the time they do it will be too late to do anything about it. They're not going to stop the show, and the audience will never know the difference. They'll think I'm you."

"Oh, Livy!" cried Cosima. "You're such a good friend!"

There was urgent knocking on the door. It was Jon. "Cosi? Cosi? They've called beginners."

Olivia nodded at her friend. "I'm just coming, Jon," said Cosi.

"You'd better be. Now! I'm going out front to join Alicia."

"Don't worry, Jon, we're on our way down. You go," called Olivia. Then she turned to Cosi. "Have you got a coat with you?" she asked.

"A coat? Why?"

"Because you can't run round the streets of London in an Edwardian nightgown, can you?"

"Where am I going?" asked Cosi.

"After the interval, you're going to go and tell Jack what you did and beg his forgiveness. Then you're going to race back here in time for the curtain call. I reckon we look so alike in our costumes that we'll get away with me pretending to be you during the performance, but when they bring the lights up for the curtain call somebody in the audience is sure to twig. So make sure you're back after confessing to Jack."

Cosi gulped.

"You did say that you'd put your head in the jaws of a crocodile if I asked you to," said Olivia. "At least we know that Jack won't eat you."

Chapter Twenty-Two

Jon slipped into a seat in the stalls between Alicia and Eel. Georgia and Aeysha were sitting on the other side of Eel. Eel's phone bleeped. She saw the message was from Olivia, read it quickly and then showed it to Georgia and Aeysha. Their eyes grew round as saucers. Eel grinned at them. This was going to be fun!

"Is everything under control, Jon?" asked Alicia.

"The show *will* go on," he said, a little over-brightly.

"You've done a good job. It's not been easy. And just remember that an audience seldom notices mistakes."

"I sometimes think the whole thing has been a mistake right from the start, although at the time it seemed such a good idea casting the Wood family."

"Well, it's certainly brought in the crowds. There's not an empty seat. Amazing for the first preview."

"Yes, it's a completely full house," said Jon, turning round to have a look. He suddenly groaned.

"What's wrong?"

"Some press and bloggers are in. Must have paid for their tickets. I've just seen a couple of arts correspondents as well as the showbiz diarist of one of the tabloids. The papers and the bulletin boards and the blogs will be passing judgement tomorrow even though it's still almost three weeks to press night when we let the critics in."

"Well, let's just hope everyone rises to the occasion, even Cosi," said Alicia as the music began and the lights began to dim.

"*Especially* Cosi," said Jon.

"Oh, I think she will," said Eel with a big grin. "I think she's going to be fantastic."

"We do too," chorused Georgia and Aeysha and they broke into giggles until Eel shot them a warning look.

Olivia and Cosi were standing in the wings with Tom. Olivia had given him a potted version of what had happened, and he had some concerns. "Are you sure this is a good idea, Liv?" he whispered again.

Olivia nodded briskly. "I've got to do it, for Cosi's sake. Anyway, it's too late to go back now. Just remember I'm not Olivia, I'm Cosi. Spread the word among the other kids. If anyone asks, they're absolutely certain that I'm Cosi. But don't tell the adults. They may try and stop us. Only Pablo knows."

The curtain swung open, the lights came up on stage and Nana could be seen, folding the children's clothes. The audience laughed. Mrs Darling appeared and went to close the nursery window and, as she did so, Cosmo's face appeared eerily at the window as if he was a ghost trying to get in. It was so spooky that the audience gasped and Mrs Darling cried, "Who are you? What do you want?" before he disappeared. Then Tom took Olivia's hand and pulled her on to the stage, and Cosi, her head bent over as she pretended to be Olivia, slipped away to where Pablo was waiting for her. He hid her out of view in the place where Olivia normally waited to fly while he continued to work frantically to adjust the rigging now that no swapping was necessary.

On stage, the lights were hot and bright. For just a second Olivia's stomach felt as if it had been popped in a tumble dryer, and then almost as quickly it settled again and she felt a surge of adrenalin. Tom squeezed her hand. Chloe Bonar caught sight of them, stared at Olivia for a beat, but without stumbling just carried on with her next line.

Then Jasper Wood appeared on stage as Mr Darling. He took no notice of the children at all, and instead concentrated on a piece of business with Mrs Darling in which she mothered him like a small child and helped him with his bow tie. The scene continued as Mr Darling suggested that it was mistake to have a dog for a nanny and Mrs Darling confessed her fears about the boy at the window. Even when Michael protested over taking some medicine and Wendy ran to get Mr Darling's medicine so he could take his, too, Jasper didn't seem to notice that the girl offering him the bottle and spoon was not his daughter.

Then the scene was over and the lights in the nursery were dimmed. Cosmo flew in through the nursery window with Tinkerbell, who, to the audience's delight, was represented by the dancing flame that had been Jack's idea. Cosmo's Peter Pan found his shadow in the chest of drawers and Olivia sat up in the bed and asked, "Boy, why are you crying?" After that the scene just sped by and Olivia forgot that she was Olivia Marvell and was instead just a girl called Wendy Darling about to fly off on the biggest adventure of her life.

In Row G of the stalls, Alicia and Jon glanced at each other. Everything was going so well. Chloe Bonar was charming, Jasper was surprisingly comic, Nana the dog was so delightful that Jon was sure they'd be inundated with letters from children offering her a home, and Cosmo was unexpectedly ethereal as if he wasn't a boy at all but a spark made by rubbing childhood and innocence together to make a flame. But it was Cosi as Wendy who was the real revelation.

Jon and Alicia leaned forward in their seats. This Wendy wasn't just the Edwardian "little mother" of Barrie's original. She had

Wendy's softness but somehow she seemed far more contemporary, infinitely more spirited, and touched by something sadder too, as if she already knew that her days in the nursery were numbered and that if she didn't fly to Never Land this very minute she never would. The audience was entranced. Both puzzled and astonished by Cosi's unexpected transformation into such a consummate actress, Alicia and Jon leaned further and further forward in their seats. Alicia's jaw suddenly dropped open. They turned to each other at the same moment.

"Are you thinking what I'm thinking?" asked Jon.

Alicia nodded. "I certainly am," she whispered.

"What's going on?" asked Jon. He went to stand up.

But Alicia placed a restraining hand on his knee and shook her head. "Leave it, Jon," she said gently but firmly. "Whatever will be will be."

"We'll have to make an announcement at the interval," hissed Jon.

"Ssh," said the man sitting behind him, who was one of *Peter Pan*'s angel investors.

Without his money, and that of his fellow angels, a production would never get off the ground. He was in a very good mood because a production and acting this good guaranteed a hit and he'd get a big return on his money. He particularly liked Cosima Wood's Wendy. That girl was a real star. "It's lovely. You're spoiling it making all this noise."

"It *is* lovely," agreed Eel in a whisper. "Cosmo is fab and Cosi is amazing." Jon stared at her. Couldn't Eel see it was her own sister up there? He went to open his mouth but Alicia gave him a look that silenced him. He sat back in his seat, deciding to enjoy the show and worry about conspiracies later.

The scene before the interval was coming to a close. Peter and Wendy were perched on Marooner's Rock in the middle of the lagoon as the waters rose threateningly around them. In a few minutes, they might both drown.

"Go, Wendy," cried Peter, placing her hand on the tail of the kite that would carry her to safety.

"I won't go without you," she cried desperately.

"You must," cried Peter. He pushed her from the rock and the kite lifted Wendy off her feet and carried her out over the auditorium, the music soaring with her. The audience gasped with pleasure, but then their attention was cleverly directed straight back to the stage where the waters were beginning to lap over the edges of the rock and Peter's feet. A huge white moon rose in the sky and the stars came out, winking against the midnight-blue backdrop.

"To die will be an awfully big adventure," cried Peter, and as he did so, a dozen mermaids appeared in the water as if by magic, the music rose to a crescendo and the curtain fell for the interval. For a moment you could have heard a pin drop and then the audience cheered and clapped loudly.

"It's fantastic, Jon. You should be very proud," said the man sitting behind them.

"It is," agreed his wife. "The Wood twins are great. Particularly Cosima. Who'd have thought from that TV show she does with her brother that she could ever be so good?"

"She's the best," piped up their children, still clapping furiously.

Olivia, who had landed in the box furthest

away from the stage, unclipped herself from her harness, and raced down to the front of the theatre and round to the stage door. Then she ran full pelt up to Cosi's dressing room where Cosi was waiting. The applause was still coming over the tannoy.

"You're brilliant, Livy. I can hear it," said Cosi.

"No, you're brilliant, Cosi," said Olivia, firmly stressing the "you". "You're giving the performance of your life."

There was a knock on the door and Tom, Cosmo, Will Todd and some of the other children crowded into the dressing room. They were all up to speed with what was happening, and happy to go along with it. They all liked and respected Olivia and as far as the Lost Boys were concerned, anything Tom said was all right by them. He was a bit of a hero in their eyes. Besides, all of them, even the very youngest, had experienced that tickle of fear that heralds stage fright and knew what might happen should the tickle get out of control.

"Watch out! I saw Jon James and Miss Swan heading this way," said the boy who played Nibs.

"Right," said Olivia. "Is everyone ready? You all know what to do?" They all nodded. "I want Oscar-winning performances from all of you. You particularly, Cosi. Don't blow it, now."

There was a sharp knock at the door and Jon James strode in, followed by Alicia, Eel, Georgia and Aeysha.

"What on earth is going on—" The director broke off. The children were surrounding Cosi and cheering her wildly.

"You were fantastic, Cosi!" said Tom.

"Inspired," said Cosmo. "Dad and I are so proud of you, sis."

"I'm very proud of you, too, Cosmo. I'm glad you're my twin." Cosi met her brother's eye and a look of understanding flashed between them. Cosmo smiled.

"You were awesome, Cosi," said Eel. "I know that Jon and Gran are really impressed."

"We are," said Alicia with a twinkle in her eye. "It's like some kind of miracle. And you too, Cosmo. You have surpassed yourself. You're a real actor." For once Cosmo seemed to be lost for words.

"Isn't Cosi good, Mr James?" said Will, turning to Jon and looking as if butter wouldn't melt in his mouth.

Before Jon could reply there was another knock on the door and Pablo walked in. "I just came up to congratulate you on your magnificent performance, Cosi. All of us on the technical side, we watch you very closely and we are very admiring of your talent," he said.

Jon looked at Pablo as if he had gone raving mad. A little smile of amusement began to play around Alicia's lips.

"Thank you," said Cosi charmingly. "All I can do is my best."

Pablo turned to Livy and gave her an almost imperceptible wink. "Your flying, Livy, it is good tonight but not as good as Cosi's acting. But you and Cosi and Cosmo are our little stars." He turned to Jon. "You must be very proud of them all."

Jon, who was feeling ever more confused, opened his mouth. "But . . . but . . ." he started.

At that moment Jasper Wood – now dressed as Captain Hook with a wig that looked like black candles had melted over his head – burst into the room without knocking and said delightedly, "No buts, Jon, it's going swell. Everybody says so. This is going to be a Wood family triumph."

The children looked at each other, and Alicia raised an eyebrow. Had Jasper really not noticed what was going on? The five-minute bell rang, signalling the end of the interval. Jasper swept Jon out of the room with him and Tom, while Cosmo and the other children followed, leaving Alicia alone with Olivia and Cosi. She looked at them both very hard.

"You do realise that what you're doing is utterly unprofessional, don't you? But no doubt you have a good explanation and I will of course expect to hear it eventually." She gave her granddaughter a piercing gaze. "But it is by any standards a most remarkable performance. Keep it up, girls." She left as the three-minute bell rang and the call went out over the tannoy for "beginners Act IV".

Cosi immediately put on her coat and pulled a hat that Pablo had lent her down over her eyes.

"Ready?" asked Olivia. "You've got the torch?"

Cosi nodded.

"You *must* be back in time for the curtain call," Olivia reminded her. "I can't carry that off.

The audience will realise I'm not you."

"Don't worry, I'll be back," said Cosi. "Do you think Jack'll be very angry with me?"

"I can't answer that," said Olivia. "All I know is that he deserves to hear from you what you did to him."

Chapter Twenty-Three

Alicia and Jon settled into their seats again. Jon had wanted to stay backstage and watch from the wings, but Alicia, with a little help from Eel, Georgia and Aeysha, had firmly steered him back to his seat.

"You realise we are colluding in a con, Alicia," hissed Jon. "We're deceiving the audience. They think they're seeing one thing and they're really seeing something else entirely. I expect we could be arrested under the Trade Descriptions Act. I really should make an announcement."

"But, Jon," said Alicia smoothly, "what would you announce?" She waved her arm around. "That all these people are having a fantastic night at the theatre and really enjoying themselves?"

Aeysha said, "My mum always says that all theatre is a kind of deception, and that it only works because the audience wants and allows itself to be deceived."

"That's why it's so magic," said Georgia with a little shiver. "The audience has to join in. We have to want it to work for it to work."

"Yes," said Eel. "When I was in *The Sound of Music* I used to think that it was like being a magician. You make people see what you want them to see, so they believe it's all magic. That's what a theatre director does too."

"The girls are right, Jon," said Alicia. "The audience enjoys the collusion so why spoil it for them by breaking the illusion and telling them how it's being done?"

Jon didn't look convinced.

"Look," continued Alicia. "If you asked that man sitting behind you whether or not he believes in fairies, he'd laugh and say of course not. But I guarantee that in half an hour's time, when Peter says that Tinkerbell is dying because she has drunk medicine poisoned by Captain Hook and the only way to save her is for everyone in the audience to say that they believe in fairies then that same man will shout that he does at the top of his voice and maybe even with a tear in his eye. I don't know what is going on tonight but maybe you should just allow yourself to believe in magic."

"Do you all believe in it?" asked Jon.

"Of course we do," chorused Eel, Georgia and Aeysha.

Then Alicia added, "Like the rest of this audience, bar possibly you, while the curtain is up I'm prepared to believe that I am watching Cosi Wood give the performance of her life. Who is to say whether it's true or just a beautiful illusion?"

"And tomorrow? What will we do at tomorrow's performance?"

"Oh, don't worry about tomorrow; tomorrow will sort itself," said Eel brightly, and she sang a snatch from *Annie*. The lights dimmed and the curtain went up to reveal the Lost Boys' home under the ground.

Cosi crept along the river path from the direction of the Swan. It was very dark and she felt a little frightened to be out on her own in such blackness. But the stars were out and she could see boats going up and down the river so although she was alone she didn't feel too far from other people. But she was pleased she had her torch. Best of all, she could see the trees. Jack had fixed up some fairy lights and she could see the banners they had put up blowing in the breeze. She knew that she had to hurry if she was going to get back to the theatre in time for the curtain call. But the closer she got to the trees and Jack, the more her feet dragged. How she dreaded telling him! It wasn't so much that she feared his anger; the thing she feared most was that he would pity her. She couldn't bear that, although pity was the best that she could hope for and more than she deserved.

She was so close now that she could see Jack moving about in the trees. He was like a monkey, entirely unconcerned about how high up he was in the branches. She so admired his physical ease. She saw him swing himself on to a zip-wire and make his way to the ground, where he had a folding chair and small picnic table with a Thermos, a book and a torch. He unscrewed the Thermos and poured himself a cup of something hot. Cosi could see the liquid steaming by the light of his torch. It was, thought

Cosi to herself, now or never. She started to step out from behind her tree but, instead of sitting, Jack put down his cup, picked up his torch and strolled away towards the bushes. She guessed he was going to relieve himself. She hung back, feeling a little bit embarrassed. She would hate to be caught spying so she turned off her torch. It was eerie standing alone in the pitch blackness.

As her eyes adjusted to the dark she noticed another figure bobbing through the trees from the other direction. The figure was torchless and running as lightly and soundlessly as a panther. She wondered whether it was a jogger. But the figure ran through the trees straight towards Jack's table and, just for a moment, picked up Jack's cup. Then he ran onwards, passing within a few trees of where Cosi was standing watching in the darkness. She held her breath and the figure passed on oblivious to her presence. What odd behaviour! For a moment Cosi had thought that whoever it was had intended to steal Jack's cup. But who would want to steal a plastic cup? Maybe, she reasoned, it was a jogger overcome with a raging thirst while out for a run. But when she thought about it, she couldn't remember seeing the figure take a drink; it had looked more as if he'd been putting something into the cup. Maybe the jogger took sugar?

She was still puzzling when she saw Jack returning from the bushes. She waited until he sat down in the chair and picked up his book. She took a deep breath. She had to speak to him, and soon. It was almost nine fifteen. She knew that around now Tinkerbell would be drinking Peter's poisoned medicine. Suddenly she realised what she had just witnessed. She saw Jack pick up the cup and raise it to his lips, and with a great screech Cosi started running towards him as fast as she could. Jack looked up in alarm as she skidded into him and knocked the cup from his hand.

"Hello, Cosi," said Jack very calmly. "It's lovely of you to pay me a visit, but shouldn't you be on stage?"

"Your drink!" said Cosi, shaking with shock. "I saw somebody put something in it." Jack looked sceptical. "I did!" she gasped. "I was hiding behind that tree and when you disappeared into those bushes somebody tampered with your cup."

Jack picked up the cup, which had fallen on the grass. Most of the coffee had drained

222

away, but a dribble remained along the side and there was a trail of white sediment behind it. His stomach lurched. This was getting serious. If Mr Wilkes-Cox was prepared to go to such lengths, somebody might get really hurt. He wondered whether Alicia was right to think there was a connection between what was going on here and the sabotage of the flying system at the theatre. He suddenly felt panicked. If Cosi was here, who was playing Wendy? He was sure he knew the answer.

"Is Liv paying Wendy?" he asked urgently and his eyes were dark with fear.

"Yes," said Cosi. "She's brilliant. But don't worry. She's completely safe. Nothing bad will happen to her. You don't have to worry about the flying. I promise. But somebody has just tried to kill you!"

Jack re-examined the sediment in the cup. "It's unlikely anyone hates me enough to want me dead. I think it's probably just crushed-up sleeping pills. Somebody must be very keen for me to get a good night's sleep. You realise what this means?"

"Yes," said Cosi. "Mr Wilkes-Cox is going to try to cut down the trees tonight."

"I thought after this morning's fiasco he'd let things rest a few days but I was wrong. I suppose that after things started to appear on the Internet he decided he had to move quickly. I'm going to need your help, Cosi. Most of the others are at the theatre and they may not get here in time."

"I'll do whatever I can," she said.

"I know you don't like heights, but if I help you, do you think you could be very brave and climb up that tree?"

Cosi gulped. Then she looked Jack straight in the eye and said, "If that's what it takes. But Livy said I had to go back to the theatre in time for the curtain call."

"I think in the circumstances Liv will understand. I reckon that here is the place you're most needed just at the moment." They walked over to the tree and Jack gave Cosi a leg up. She scrambled on to the first branch. For a moment she felt dizzy, as if she was going to fall, but then she moved upwards again and it became easier. Jack was shining his torch to show her where the handholds were. Then he climbed up behind her, passed her with great agility, and clambered on to a small platform he'd erected.

He reached down a hand and helped her up. Then he turned off his torch so they were sitting in darkness so complete they were unable to see each other's faces.

"In a minute we need to start texting the others," he said quietly. "But first, do you want to tell me why you're not playing Wendy and why you've come to see me? I imagine it wasn't just a spur-of-the-moment social visit?"

Cosi swallowed very hard in the dark. She was finding it difficult to speak.

"Livy isn't just playing Wendy," whispered Cosi. "She's pretending to be me playing Wendy."

"Ah," said Jack. For a moment there was silence. Then he said, "Stage fright?"

Cosi was so surprised that she almost fell out of the tree. "How did you know?"

"I experienced it once myself. On the high-wire. It was awful. Like being frozen inside, made of ice and fear not flesh and blood. I thought that if I had to walk any further I'd die and I'd have done absolutely anything to avoid having to take another step."

"That's exactly how I felt about tonight. I really believed I'd die. It felt as if there was a crocodile out in the darkness waiting to gobble me up. Oh, Jack, I've been dreading it so much." She looked at him, and could just make out his face in the gloom. "But you're amazing on the wire! How did you get over it?"

"You never really get over it," said Jack. "It's always there, perched on your shoulder like a black crow cawing in your ear. But you learn to live with it and use it to your advantage. Of course, you have to love walking the high-wire or acting enough to get past it. I don't think you like acting at all, do you? In fact, I think you hate it with a passion."

There was a long pause while Cosi nodded, before realising that Jack couldn't see her in the dark.

"I've got a confession," she said. "I did something really terrible."

"It's all right, Cosi, you don't need to tell me," replied Jack quietly. "I know."

"How?"

"From what you've just told me, and the fact you're so certain Liv is safe on the flying rig. I thought this afternoon you were trying to confess something to me. I should have realised something was up when you were so interested in how the flying system worked."

"I'm so sorry," said Cosi.

"I believe you. You've been very brave coming here tonight. And if you hadn't, I would have drunk whatever stuff was in that cup. I'd say we're quits."

Cosi smiled with relief. In the distance they heard a sudden roar of engines. Jack got out his phone and began texting. They could see the glare of headlights as the diggers and bulldozers started to roll towards them.

"Right," said Jack. "Looks like it's just you and me."

Chapter Twenty-Four

The curtain opened for the start of Act V and, as Olivia had predicted, when the pirate ship sailed into view, the audience gasped at how real it looked.

"A beautiful illusion," muttered Jon under his breath, but by now he was grinning. It was clear that *Peter Pan* was going to be a huge success. Even the famously grumpy arts correspondent of a serious national newspaper had been heard loudly declaring he believed in fairies, and when the pirates stole Wendy and the Lost Boys away, the tabloid showbiz columnist had been hissing along with the rest of the crowd.

Jasper stood on the deck of the *Jolly Roger* and began Captain Hook's famous speech: "How still the night is, nothing sounds alive. . ." The evening had been going swimmingly. Although he'd never admit it, Jasper had began to wonder if he'd made a mistake in signing up the entire family for *Peter Pan*. He'd thought Cosima was going to let them all down. But she'd surprised everyone tonight, and Cosmo was getting lots of praise too. If *Peter Pan* was a triumph perhaps they could go to Broadway and do *The Tempest* together. He'd always wanted to play Prospero. Cosmo would be a great Ariel and, although she was a little young for it, Cosi could be Miranda.

Michael, John and the Lost Boys were about to walk the plank.

"Bring up Wendy so she can watch them go to their doom," cried Hook.

Olivia was pushed up the stairs.

"So, my beauty," said Jasper with a dreadful laugh. "You are to see your children walk the plank." He did a double take.

"Are they to die?" quavered Olivia, entirely unperturbed by Jasper's reaction.

"Cosi?" hissed Jasper, forgetting where he was for a moment.

"Definitely Cosi," whispered Olivia quickly, and she turned to the boys. "I have a message from your real mothers: We hope our sons will die like English gentlemen."

The Lost Boys cheered.

"Impressive," whispered Jasper, grasping immediately that it was not in the interests of the Wood family for the truth ever to come out.

"Like father, like daughter," replied Olivia calmly, under cover of all the cheering, and Jasper thought of the YouTube clip of Cosi he'd watched earlier. Cosi was braver than ever he could be. He gave Olivia a quick wink and then they both carried on with the scene as if nothing had happened.

The show was reaching its end. The children had flown back from Never Land to the Darling nursery and been reunited with their delighted parents, and now the coda was being played in which many years later Peter Pan returns to the nursery where the grown-up Wendy now watches over her own daughter, Jane.

"Come with me to Never Land," said Peter, oblivious to the fact that the long years have passed and although he has stayed just the same, Wendy has not.

"I can't come, Peter. I've forgotten how to fly," said Wendy.

Alicia shifted in her seat. The audience might believe that they were watching Cosi Wood, but Alicia knew she was watching her granddaughter, and wearing grown-up clothes Olivia looked so much like Toni it was almost unbearable.

"I'll teach you again," said Peter, blowing fairy dust on her.

"You're wasting your time," replied Wendy sadly. Olivia's eyes glistened with tears.

"Why?"

"Because I am no longer young. I've grown up. I couldn't help it," replied Wendy. "That little girl is my baby."

"What does she call you?" asked Peter fiercely.

"Mother," whispered Wendy.

Alicia's eyes spilled tears and she was not the only one in the audience. Every adult was recalling their own lost childhood, and every child was thinking how much they would love to fly away to Never Land to frolic with the mermaids in the sparkling lagoon under endless blue sky. The scene drew to its conclusion as Wendy's daughter flew away with Peter Pan, and as the curtain fell so did the tears in the

231

audience. There was a charged silence, and then the audience began to roar their approval.

Olivia was oblivious to the response. She was scanning the wings for Cosi, a look of panic on her face.

"Where is she?" she demanded. The other children looked around helplessly. There was no sign of Cosi. "She promised she'd be back. I can't take the curtain call. I won't get away with it. Somebody in the front row is sure to notice I'm not Cosi. What are we going to do?" The audience were cheering as the pirates ran on to take their bow.

"I can't go out there!" wailed Olivia.

"It'll be more suspicious if you don't, Liv," said Tom, taking her hand firmly. "If anyone in the audience has the slightest hunch that something funny is going on, Wendy's absence at the curtain call will only confirm it. Jon said there were press out there. If they get a sniff of this, it'll be all over the front pages tomorrow."

"This is a disaster. She can't do anything right," said Olivia irritably.

Pablo hurried up to them, looking agitated. "No sign of Cosi?"

Olivia shook her head angrily.

"You've got to take the curtain call, Livy. I've spoken to the guys on lighting. They'll keep it all really low. Take the grips out of your hair and push it forward to keep your face covered. You and Cosmo should take your bow from the back of stage. One curtain only, then Jasper will take the limelight. Don't come forward to join him until the whole cast do, and then, Tom, make sure you and the others hide her as much as you can. However much they stamp and cheer we're going to cut the final curtain short." He pushed them towards the stage. . .

The curtain swished closed for the final time. The lengthy applause finally died away as the audience realised it wasn't going to rise again however much noise they made. Olivia looked around agitatedly from her position at the back of the stage. She was certain they had got away with it. But where was Cosi? Why hadn't she turned up for the curtain call? Irritation had turned to worry and a real fear that something had happened to her friend. She hoped that Cosi hadn't run away rather than face up to what she'd done. Tom had Olivia by the arm and was bundling her up the stairs with Cosmo. It was like being arrested.

"We've got to get you changed and out of the building before Jon comes round and demands to see Cosi. We can just say that you've both gone. Hurry!"

They left her in the dressing room where she started quickly pulling on her own clothes. Suddenly there was a frantic banging on the door. She jumped in shock.

"Livy, Livy, it's me, Eel!"

Olivia unlocked the door and her little sister tumbled into the room.

"Livy! I've had a message from Jack. Cosi's at the Swan with him. We've got to get round there. Mr Wilkes-Cox is back with his diggers. The battle for the trees has begun."

Olivia felt the adrenalin surge through her once more. "Go and tell everyone, including Pablo, and get moving," she said, pulling on her trainers. "I'll meet you there."

Eel ran towards the door just as it opened and Alicia walked in, swiftly followed by Jasper. She squeaked and shot Olivia a look of sympathy before scooting off down the corridor.

"Jon's been held up talking to the press but he wants to talk to you and Cosi right away," said Alicia gravely. "And I want a word with you both too. Where is she?"

Olivia swallowed. "She's at the Swan with Jack. Mr Wilkes-Cox has come back to cut the trees down."

"So that explains the bizarre curtain call," said Alicia. "You were lucky to get away with it. Now, I can't condone what has gone on tonight—"

Jasper put up his hand to cut her off. "I want to thank you, Olivia Marvell. I think you've done Cosi a good turn tonight," he said. Before he could continue, they heard Jon's voice in the corridor.

The two adults looked at each other and seemed to reach a decision.

"Quick," said Alicia, opening the window and peering out. "It's not far down to that ledge and then beyond that to the ground. I'm sure you're manage, Livy."

Olivia grinned. "But you're always telling me not to do dangerous things, Gran," she said as she clambered out of the window.

"I make exceptions when it's absolutely necessary," said Alicia, slamming the window shut just as Jon walked into the room.

"Where are they?" he demanded.

"Who?" asked Alicia, a picture of innocence. Jon just looked at her. "Olivia went back to the Swan after the interval to see Jack, and I'm afraid you've just missed Cosi."

"That's right," said Jasper. "Cosi was so sorry she had to go without seeing you. She and all the other children have gone to the Swan. But it was such a pleasure acting opposite my daughter tonight. She was flawless."

"Yes," said Alicia. "The whole thing was a triumph. When word gets out, *Peter Pan* is going to be a smash. You should be delighted, Jon."

Jon opened his mouth but at that moment the stage manager arrived and announced that the BBC wanted to interview him straightaway. He left, muttering darkly under his breath.

"Your Olivia is a fine actress," said Jasper softly. "So generous too in what she's done for my daughter tonight. Do you know why she did it?"

"I can guess but I think you need to ask Cosi that," said Alicia. Then she added, "You've got to let Cosi go, Jasper. She doesn't want to be part of the Wood family dynasty. Children have to find their own path in the world. You'll still have Cosmo. He enjoys acting, and he was very good tonight. Almost as good as Livy. He's come on brilliantly. Set Cosi free and she'll fly. I'm certain of it."

"You're absolutely right, Alicia," said Jasper. "I'm beginning to realise I've clipped Cosi's wings too much. She needs her childhood back before it's gone forever."

Alicia smiled. "Now, I must get back to the Swan and find out what's happening with the trees."

"I'll come with you," said Jasper. "I want to do anything I can to help."

Chapter Twenty-Five

The bulldozers and diggers rumbled over the uneven ground towards the trees, their bright lights making Jack and Cosi screw up their eyes against the dazzle. They stopped a hundred metres or so from the trees with their engines gently idling. Cosi felt something inside her, a tickle of possibility, as if she was at the start of something completely new in her life.

"Come down from the trees!" shouted Mr Wilkes-Cox through a loud hailer. "Do not put yourselves at risk. You cannot stop us. We have permission to cut down the trees, and the law is on our side. We will use it if you resist, and you may get hurt. Please come down."

"Are you ready, Cosi?" shouted Jack over the noise.

"Yes!" she shouted back and she felt as if she'd grown to about three times her normal size.

"I might have to leave you here and use the zip-wires to go and defend other trees, if necessary. There's only so much we can do from just one tree on our own."

"No problem, Jack," said Cosi. "I'll be OK here. I know what I've got to do."

"I am going to count to ten," shouted Mr Wilkes-Cox. "If you have not come down from the trees by then, the bulldozers will move in." To Mr Wilkes-Cox's surprise, Jack and Cosi took up the count. They seemed so confident but how could just one man and a girl defend all those trees by themselves? He had expected that they would give up without a fight when they realised what they were up against, and he was counting on Jack starting to feel very sleepy any time soon.

"... eight ... nine ... ten ...!" shouted Jack and Cosi in unison with Mr Wilkes-Cox.

"Come and get us!" called Cosi, laughing loudly like a child playing a game. Mr Wilkes-Cox was so furious that he nodded towards one of the bulldozers, which began edging towards the tree where Cosi and Jack were sitting. *That'll frighten them down*, thought Mr Wilkes-Cox. The bulldozer rolled closer.

"Hold your nerve, Cosi!" warned Jack. The machine moved towards the tree and when it was just a few metres away Cosi and Jack turned on the high-pressure hoses they'd been keeping out of sight and aimed them straight at the windscreen.

The driver couldn't see anything and a few seconds later he could see even less as a bag of flour broke against the windscreen and flour splattered everywhere. The bulldozer ground to a halt.

Mr Wilkes-Cox gritted his teeth and nodded to two of the other diggers. They roared into life and trundled menacingly towards the tree. The same thing happened. This time the drivers leapt out of their cabs only to be drenched with water. They were getting very angry. Three pieces of equipment were now out of commission because of the sticky mix of water and flour across the windscreens. Using the windscreen wipers simply smeared the mess across the glass.

Mr Wilkes-Cox, drenched and splattered

with flour so that he resembled a deranged zombie, retreated a little distance away to where Bill Jukes was standing watching. "There's only two of them, so they can't defend every single tree in the line because they haven't got the reach," advised Bill. "Try and take out the trees at the far sides."

Mr Wilkes-Cox shouted and pointed and one of the diggers headed towards the trees at the far end of the row, beyond where Jack and Cosi's hosepipes could do any damage. But no sooner had it headed that way than Jack set off on the wires he'd strung over the tops of the trees. Jack was fast and agile while the digger had to negotiate the uneven ground. Jack reached the farthest tree at the same time as the digger and immediately started spraying it with water before following that up with two well-aimed bags of flour. They split across the windscreen in a pleasing exploding-star formation. The driver couldn't see where he was going so he leapt out of the cab and ran away but not before he too was targeted with flour and water.

Another digger began to roll towards the tree, while on the far side another was heading towards the tree furthest from Jack, right at the other end of the row. Jack looked around desperately. He couldn't be in two places at once. Cosi had just disabled another bulldozer but the men were busy washing the gunk off some of the others and they'd soon be back in commission. She was doing a fantastic job in the middle, but she couldn't get to the far end of the row where a digger had almost reached one of the trees and already had its jaws wide open.

Jack pelted the nearest digger with flour and turned to start clambering back towards the threatened tree at the other end of the row. An astonishing sight met his eyes. Cosi had leapt off the platform where she'd been standing and was whizzing down the zip-wire to the next one. She landed with a thud, but didn't stop. She simply picked up the hose resting there and sprayed water all over the digger before landing a bag of flour on its windscreen in a perfect bull's eye. Jack reached her just as another digger started to approach.

"I'm so proud of you, Cosi," he shouted. "That was an amazingly brave thing for someone who is afraid of heights to do."

"I remembered what you said, Jack," gasped Cosi as she flung another bag of flour at the digger. "If you care enough about something you learn to live with your fear and use it to your advantage."

Jack looked around. "We're not going to be able to hold out much longer on our own."

"So it's just as well that the cavalry has arrived," shouted Cosi as the Swan children, led by Olivia, Tom and Pablo, ran into view and were soon swarming all over the trees.

Chapter Twenty-Six

"I'm afraid," said Police Inspector Slightly rather sadly, "that I've looked at the documents and it appears that Mr Wilkes-Cox and Mr Jukes here are telling the truth. They do have the right to remove these trees. Mr Jukes is in charge of planning and he has approved the application. The papers have an official stamp, which makes it all legal. They are only trying to do what they are entitled to do, so I'm afraid I'm going to have to ask you all to come down from the trees and let them get on with their job."

There was real regret in his voice. He thought that the trees were very beautiful, but the law was the law, and although Mr Wilkes-Cox seemed a nasty piece of work and Bill Jukes a little shifty, if they had the law on their side there was nothing he could do to stop them. It was a pity, and what was even more of a pity was that, if the celebrities refused to come down from the trees, he would have to arrest them for obstruction and that would make asking for their autographs a bit tricky. Mrs Slightly and the children had been begging him to buy tickets to see that new West End production of *Peter Pan*, and life might not be worth living if he told them that he had had to arrest the stars and most of the cast. Although she was looking a little dishevelled and covered in flour, he was sure that he also recognised that pretty Chloe Bonar from off the telly too.

When reinforcements had arrived, in the shape of Olivia and the others, the tide had soon turned. By the time Georgia, Aeysha, Kasha and some of the other Swan pupils turned up, Mr Wilkes-Cox and the diggers were in full retreat. The Swans started celebrating their victory and congratulating Jack and Cosi on doing such a good job.

"I couldn't believe it when I saw you on the zip-wire between trees," said Olivia to Cosi. "You're a real hero."

"She really is," said Jack and Jasper

simultaneously. Cosi's face lit up with joy to hear her dad talking about her like that.

Mr Wilkes-Cox was just mounting a second attack when they heard the distant sound of sirens and within seconds three police cars had arrived. The policemen, who had had a long, very tiring day investigating several reports that a crocodile was loose on the streets of London, were rather bemused by the sight that had met their eyes: an entire landscape covered in what looked like flour, a dozen abandoned diggers and bulldozers and lots of people who looked as if they'd just been caught in a sudden snowstorm.

They had called for reinforcements and Inspector Slightly had arrived shortly afterwards. He had studied the pieces of paper that Mr Wilkes-Cox had thrust into his hand and eventually pronounced that Jack, Olivia and the others must abandon the trees. He was inclined to believe Alicia when she had told him about the threatening phone calls she'd been receiving but she had been unable to provide any evidence. He had no choice but to act within the letter of the law and remove the protestors.

"No," cried Cosi, sitting down on a branch.

"I won't move. You'll have to remove me by force."

"Us too," cried Cosmo and Jasper.

"I'm not going anywhere," shouted Tom.

Jack had his mobile out and was texting furiously. "Who are you texting, Dad?" asked Eel.

"Some journalists," said Jack. "I spoke to them this afternoon, and although they said environmental issues weren't really front-page news they said to get back to them if something big happened. Well, this is as big as it gets: the all-star cast of *Peter Pan* in a stand-off with the police as they refuse to give way to tree vandals. I can see the headlines now."

Inspector Slightly was beginning to look very stressed. He called for back-up and was waiting for it to arrive. It looked as if it might be a long night ahead. He was worried. The law might be the law, but it wouldn't reflect well on the police if they were seen to be removing children from trees so that those trees could be cut down, particularly as he agreed with the protestors.

He had a talk with Mr Wilkes-Cox and tried to persuade him that he should abandon his attempt to cut down the trees that night, but the man had been adamant that he wanted to continue. The last straw was when two journalists and a photographer turned up, followed swiftly by a camera crew and TV reporter. The reporter and the journalists had clambered into the trees and were now conducting interviews with Jack, Jasper, Cosi and Cosmo, while the camera crew was filming the children. Eel was performing arabesques while perched on a branch and Tom was doing some daredevil stuff on the zip-wire. Pablo was also attracting a lot of attention by doing a routine on one of the trapezes. Then another TV crew turned up.

More police arrived, some with dogs. The children started to clap and sing "How Much is That Doggie in the Window?" Kasha kept throwing the dogs treats he kept in his back pocket for his puppy, which just made the animals overexcited. The children had now all linked arms and were singing "It's a Hard Knock Life – for Trees", and everyone had clapped and cheered when Ric Nighthall turned up in his Nana costume and made everyone laugh, including all of the policemen, who showed every sign of siding with the children.

Mr Wilkes-Cox was getting very impatient. He started shouting, "It's a complete circus!" at Inspector Slightly, who had decided that Mr Wilkes-Cox was deeply unpleasant.

The inspector sighed again. It was time to stop the mayhem. He picked up the loud hailer so he could be heard over the din and shouted: "Quiet, please! I'm asking you to come down now or I will have no choice but to send my men in to remove you all. I don't want to do this but you will leave me with no choice. Please come down."

The grown-ups looked at each other. It was one thing holding out against Mr Wilkes-Cox, and a completely different one to hold out against the police. They all knew that Inspector Slightly was not bluffing, and they couldn't put the children at risk. They had made their point, they had done their best, but there was nothing more they could do. The law had got the better of them. Slowly they began to make their way down from the trees, coaxing the children along. Some of the children were crying. Pablo and Tom were helping them down.

Mr Wilkes-Cox nodded at one of the workmen, who fired up an engine.

"Mr Wilkes-Cox, please," said Inspector Slightly firmly. "There are still some children in the trees." Cosi was sitting on a high branch, sobbing uncontrollably. Jack climbed up towards her.

"We've failed," she cried. "We've let the trees down."

"Cosi," said Jack, "I have to ask you to come down, because that is the responsible thing to do." Then he grinned at her. "But of course you must make up your own mind what you're going to do. I can't order you. You're not my daughter."

She looked at him, then stood up in the tree and cried, "Cock a doodle doo! Cock a doodle doo!"

Jack slid quickly down the tree and went to talk to Inspector Slightly. "I did my best to persuade her to come down, Inspector, but I think it best if you go up there yourself and talk to her."

Inspector Slightly looked up at Cosi. He hadn't climbed a tree since he was a boy. He put a foot on the lowest branch.

Mr Wilkes-Cox suddenly completely lost patience. He leapt into the cab of a bulldozer, turned on the engine and started to drive it towards the tree. Everyone scattered, and as the machine rolled forwards, a small figure appeared out of the darkness shouting, "Stop! Stop!" Everyone turned towards the figure, who ran past them all and straight into the path of the bulldozer.

"Katie!" yelled Mr Wilkes-Cox, jamming the brake on just in time. He jumped out of the cab. "What are you doing here?"

She ignored him and walked up to Inspector Slightly who was now perched on a tree branch, and thrust some papers into his hand.

"Read these," she demanded. Inspector Slightly quickly scanned the documents. "I finally found the password for Dad's e-mail account. He didn't outbid Miss Swan for that building; he bribed Bill Jukes to let him have it for almost nothing, and he's been paying someone to put the frighteners on her too. Even the authorisation to cut down the trees is false."

Inspector Slightly had finished scanning the e-mails. He jumped down from the tree and turned to Mr Wilkes-Cox and Bill Jukes. "I am arresting you on charges of conspiracy to defraud, and for bribery, corruption and harassment," he said. "You must accompany me to the station."

A great cheer went up from the crowd. Bill Jukes looked frightened. Mr Wilkes-Cox gave a great roar of rage and then went very quiet. His eyes glittered murderously as he stared at Katie as he was led away. Olivia put her arm around her, and Tom, Aeysha and Georgia all gave her a hug. Alicia came over too, and wrapped her arms around her.

Up in the tree, Cosi watched the police retreat, gave a great whoop of joy and a cock a doodle doo then started to speed down the zip-wire towards the ground. She misjudged her landing and as she hit the ground there was a loud crack. For a second, her face contorted with pain, and then she said brightly, "Oops! I think I've broken my leg."

Chapter Twenty-Seven

Not long after the arrests, an ambulance arrived to take Cosi to hospital. Jasper went with her, and Jack, Olivia, Cosmo and Tom followed in a taxi. Cosmo had really wanted Tom to come. It was confirmed by X-ray that Cosi had broken her leg, and the ward sister was astonished when everybody, including Cosi, cheered loudly at the news. She thought these theatre and circus people were very strange. The sister told Jack off again but her eyes were laughing and she blushed as she did it. Jack grinned back.

While they were waiting for Cosi's leg to be plastered, Jasper took her hands between his and told her how sorry he was that he had forced her into acting throughout her childhood years.

"Well, at least I'm out of *Peter Pan*," said Cosi cheerfully.

"You're out of acting, period, if that's what you want," said Jasper. "I was wrong in putting the family name before my family. I've not behaved well, but I hope I've learned my lesson." He suddenly looked very sad. "I've not told you this before, and I'm not telling you to try and excuse my behaviour but because I want you to understand what motivated me." He took a deep breath. "It's because of my brother."

"But you always said you were an only child, Dad," said Cosmo, surprised.

"I was after the age of eight. I had an elder brother, David. He was the talented one. Everyone said what a great future he had as an actor. He played Peter Pan. He was captivating. He was thirteen when he died in a skating accident. My parents never got over it. He was their pride and joy; he was the one who was going to carry on the Wood family name and become a great actor. Everyone said so. After David died, I vowed to myself that I would do it instead and that my kids would, too. It was a silly promise, and I hope you'll both forgive me because I can never forgive myself."

There was a silence like a sliver of glass, and then Cosi said, "Come here, Dad, and give me a hug." Jasper moved into her arms and she continued. "I was wrong when I said that you were like Captain Hook. You're much more like Mr Darling. Mine and Cosmo's very own Mr Darling."

She suddenly looked very serious. "I've got a confession too, Dad. I did something terrible," she said, glancing at Jack.

But Jack cut in, "There's no need for anyone else to know, Cosi. That's between you and me, and it's over. If you want to tell people, that's fine, it's your decision, but as far as I'm concerned no more need ever be said."

Cosi smiled at him gratefully. Just then Alicia drew breath and everyone turned to look at her. Her face was stern and Olivia felt her heart begin to thump. She was in for a telling-off.

"You do realise, Olivia, that what you and Cosi did at the theatre tonight was deception?" said her gran. Both Olivia and Cosi felt chastened by her serious tone and they nodded.

"What you did, and I'm including you in this, Tom, was very serious and entirely unprofessional and I very much hope that nothing like it will ever happen again."

Cosi shook her head.

"It won't, Gran," whispered Olivia.

"Good," said Alicia. "So nobody need ever say anything about it ever again to anybody."

Olivia and Cosi nodded vigorously.

"And I'd just like to say," added Alicia, a twinkle coming into her eye, "how delightful it is that Cosi has the heart of a brave lion and that Livy is as great an actress as her mother."

Olivia felt very warm inside. She knew she wanted to do more acting. Playing Wendy had given her a taste for it. It was strange – she didn't mind people watching her on stage, but seeing everyone looking at her now made her feel really shy.

"Hey, Cosi, I've got a present for you," she said suddenly and she pulled out the polar bear badge.

"That's so cute!" said Cosi. "I'll never take it off. Thank you." She beamed at Olivia and Tom, and burst out happily: "I just love having friends!"

"Me too," piped up Cosmo. He blushed. "I want to apologise to everyone for being so rude

256

to you all when we first met."

"Forget it, Cosmo. It's all water under the bridge," said Tom. "Do you want to come back to the Swan later? Liv, Jack and I could give you your first taste of walking the wire?"

Cosmo looked thrilled, then glanced at his dad as if he expected him to protest. But Jasper just said cheerily, "Go for it, kiddo. I know you're in the safest possible hands."

"You know," said Cosi, "when my leg's mended I think I might like to have a go at wire-walking." Everyone cheered.

Just then Jon turned up at the hospital with a big bunch of flowers.

"Look at this," he said, showing them the front pages of two of the early editions of the Sunday papers. The first headline read: "Wood family take to the Trees". The second read: "An Awfully Big Adventure", and below was an ecstatic review of *Peter Pan*, plus an account of the battle for the trees. "It says here," said Jon, looking directly at Olivia as he spoke, "that Cosi Wood has the potential to be one of the greatest actors of her generation."

Olivia shook her head and said, "How nice, Cosi. It's such a pity that your broken leg means you'll not be able to repeat your performance."

Jon kept looking very hard at Olivia. "Is there no possibility that it could happen again?"

"Afraid not, Jon," she said, holding his gaze. "Looks like it was a one-off. But Petal will be fantastic in the role."

It was just over a week since the night of the Battle for the Trees, as it had become known. Olivia took a deep breath and blew out the thirteen candles on her cake and made a wish. It was strange being thirteen. It didn't feel any different from being twelve. But she would never be twelve again. She was a teenager! When she had first come to the Swan, the children in Year Nine had seemed so old, but next term she would be in Year Nine too. She grinned at Tom, who smiled back. She cut the cake and started to hand it out.

"None for you, Cosmo, is that right?" she said with a grin. His face dropped. "But I thought you were wheat-free?" she said.

"Not any more. That was in the days when I was talent-free too."

"Those days aren't over, Cosmo, no way!" shouted Cosi from the sofa where she was laid up with her leg in plaster. Everyone laughed and Cosmo threw a cushion at her.

"Katie?" asked Olivia.

"Yes, please, Livy," said Katie shyly. After everything that had happened over the last few days she felt overwhelmed to be sitting here with Olivia and her friends. She was squashed between Aeysha and Georgia, who kept smiling at her, and Tom was treating her as if she was one of the gang. They were all being so kind to her. She still felt guilty about what she'd done to her father, although Inspector Slightly, Alicia and even her mum, who had started divorce proceedings, kept telling her she'd done the right thing.

It turned out that Alicia hadn't been the only person Mr Wilkes-Cox had been harassing. He had bought some little terraced houses and had been illegally trying to evict the sitting tenants, including several families and a ninety-year-old couple. They had been terrified by him but were prepared to give evidence against him in court. Then, just when it was almost certain that he would have been going to prison for a very long time, he had skipped bail and fled abroad.

Katie was very worried about her and her mum's future. It turned out that their mansion was mortgaged up to the hilt and would soon be repossessed. Alicia saw Katie's wan face and made up her mind what to do. She would consult with Olivia and her friends, but if they were all happy about it, which she was sure they would be, she would offer Katie a scholarship so she could return to the Swan after the summer holidays.

Olivia looked at all her presents and cards.

"Open mine, open mine," said Eel, handing Olivia an envelope. It was two tickets to the ballet to see *Coppélia* at the Royal Opera House.

Olivia laughed. "Thank you, Eel, for giving me the present you wanted," she said, giving her sister a kiss. "I assume you will be coming with me?"

Eel nodded enthusiastically. "I was worried you wouldn't ask, and take somebody else. I'd already told Tom and the others to refuse if you asked them." Everyone laughed.

Olivia opened all her other presents and cards, which included a beautiful book of photographs of trapeze artists from Pablo, some exquisite vellum-covered notebooks from Alicia

260

and a first edition of *Peter Pan* from Jasper, Cosi and Cosmo.

Tom, Aeysha and Georgia had bought her chocolates and a framed photograph that Tom had taken of her flying during a rehearsal. Finally there was just a box-shaped gift left on the table. Olivia knew that it was from Jack. She unwrapped it carefully. Inside was a small box and as she eased off the lid, the sides of the box fell away to reveal an exquisite model of a miniature Big Top. When Olivia peered inside there was dark-haired girl walking the high-wire and on the other end of the wire opposite her was a man.

"Oh, Jack, it's so beautiful," she said, tears springing to her eyes. "Did you make it yourself?" He nodded. She looked at him shyly and said, "It's you and me, isn't it?"

Jack nodded again. "Liv, chick," he said. "A very long time ago, in what seems like another life, I asked if you would like to be my partner on the high-wire. It never happened because of my accident. I know that in the meantime you've found another partner in Tom, and I don't want to upset that relationship at all. But Tom's committed to *Peter Pan* for a good few weeks yet, so I wondered whether you and I might work up a double act together. Would you like that?"

Olivia was so choked up that she could hardly speak, and just nodded instead.

"Good," said Jack, "because we've already got a gig. We're going to the Edinburgh Festival Fringe during the summer. We can all be together as a family, and you and I can walk the high-wire at the heart of the show. It's time the Swan Circus hit the road!"

"The Swan Circus!" gasped Olivia.

"Yes," said Alicia. "Your dad and Pablo and I have been planning it for weeks. I think it's a wonderful idea. The Swan is going to Edinburgh. We should toast its success." She raised her glass. "To the Swan Circus!"

"To the Swan Circus!" chorused everyone.

"To the Swan Circus at the Edinburgh Festival," whispered Olivia, a little after everyone else. She raised her glass up high and her eyes were shining like stars.

To find out about further titles in the

Olivia

series and other upcoming Nosy Crow books
visit

www.nosycrow.com

To read an extract from

Olivia's
Enchanted Summer

turn the page!

nosy
crow

Chapter One

Olivia Marvell stood by the railings at the top of the Mound and looked down over Edinburgh. Below her was a group of acrobats attempting a human pyramid and wobbling dangerously like a badly-set jelly on a hot summer's day. Two teenage girls were doing a comic juggling act. One of them was juggling perfectly with what appeared to be half a dozen fresh eggs, but which Olivia suspected were rubber fakes. The other girl was throwing real eggs into the air and failing to catch them. They kept splatting on her partner's head, whose pretend anger was creating much hilarity amongst the crowd.

There was also a troupe of mad tap-dancers wearing kilts who were doing an intricate routine to bagpipes and being cheered enthusiastically. Olivia smiled as she watched some small children trying to join in and falling over their own – and the dancers' – feet. She felt a mounting sense of excitement as if someone were hugging her insides very tightly.

Below her a mass of people swirled, all attracted to the Mound and its merry sights and sounds on this bright early August afternoon just a few days before the official start of the Edinburgh Festival Fringe. It made Olivia think of the Pied Piper. It was as if the entire world was being drawn towards the city by an invisible thread of music and bright colours. She wished her friend Tom was here to see it, but he was finishing his contract playing John in a huge sell-out West End production of *Peter Pan* and wouldn't be free until the very end of August.

Olivia wheeled round as somebody touched her shoulder. It was Georgia and Aeysha.

"Hey!" she said, pleased to see her friends. "Did you get rid of all your posters?"

"All but one," said Aeysha, unfurling a midnight blue A3 sheet dotted with silver stars. It showed a girl on a trapeze surrounded by fairies and a magician and a sprite walking the high wire. Emblazoned across the top in small golden gothic letters were the words: "The Swan Circus Presents" and then in even bigger letters it read: "*Enchantment*: a Magical Circus Entertainment." They had all looked at the poster many times before but it still made Olivia feel shivery with pleasure.

"Eel and I found people to take all ours," she said. "Lots of shops will put them up in their windows. It helps that they're so striking. The woman in one of the cafes said she might even come and see our show after Eel did a crazy tap dance and stood on her head. I can't wait to put the Swan circus in front of an audience!"

She grinned at her friends and they grinned back. Aeysha winked and Georgia did a little skip. Olivia didn't have to say anything; she could tell from Georgia's doll-like face and Aeysha's sparkling eyes with their thick dark lashes that they felt as excited as she did.

Look out for more fabulous fiction
from Nosy Crow!

Coming soon...